HER DRAGON SAVIOR
AWAKEN THE DRAGON

MILLY TAIDEN
AVA HUNTER

HER DRAGON SAVIOR
AWAKEN THE DRAGON 1

*NEW YORK TIMES and USA TODAY
BESTSELLING AUTHOR*
MILLY TAIDEN

&

AVA HUNTER

This book is a work of fiction. The names, characters, places, and incidents are fictitious or have been used fictitiously, and are not to be construed as real in any way. Any resemblance to persons, living or dead, actual events, locales, or organizations is entirely coincidental.

Published By
Milly Taiden & Ava Hunter
http://millytaiden.com
http://avahunterbooks.com
Her Dragon Savior
Copyright © 2021 by Milly Taiden & Ava Hunter
Cover: Jacqueline Sweet
All Rights Are Reserved. No part of this book may be used or reproduced in any manner whatsoever without written permission, except in the case of brief quotations embodied in critical articles and reviews.

Property of Milly Taiden & Ava Hunter
May 2021

❀ Created with Vellum

ABOUT THE BOOK

Dragon-shifter Evair awakens to an attack and is wounded as he defends himself. He's drawn to a beautiful but strong-willed witch who helps him control his power and shifting abilities. But he's much more interested in finding out how to make her his. And once he gets a taste of her, he knows he's never letting her go.

Penelope can't believe the gorgeous dragon needs her. She's happy to teach him about the new world and help him figure out why he was woken. Love and romance weren't in the cards. She tries to fight it, but their bond is stronger than she realized. Are they mates? Could he be right? His flaming kisses and warm caresses make her hope he is.

A group of poachers is hunting down Evair's kind. It's a race against time to get to them before they kill more of his people. Love blooms in the midst of their battles. Their love will either survive or die crushed in their war for survival.

—For dragon lovers. We love them too!

Enjoy

1
EVAIR

There was a low rumble.

Like something so ancient, so mythic, it was impossible to grasp how it could burst upon the world, but it spun like a top somewhere near the core of the Earth and gained in strength. The ground above split. Rich dark earth bursting forth as the green meadows hewed back to give way.

Then, like a beacon rising from the deepest, most secret bowels of the world, a glitter broke forth. After so many centuries buried, the dust of ages fell away, and the pinnacle glistened in the sun. A spiral of pure, untarnished gold set with a ruby broke free and surged up toward the sky.

It rose as a monolith, sending cascades of soil

tumbling back and snapping the roots of grandfather trees like sinews of felled deer. When at last the whole of it broke free into the air, the rumbling stopped. An eerie calm settled in the wake of the roar, lending even more majesty to the eruption. Settled on the Earth but reaching for the sky, this jewel-studded spire towered over the countryside, a wonder to eyes that had never known its glory.

The Dragon Shrine.

It had lain in darkness for hundreds of years. So long that it had faded from fact and wrapped itself in the unsullied mantle of legend. All who had known it before were gone. Dead from age, and sickness, and war, and all the things that mortals die from. Returned to the ground to nourish it, only leaving behind the memories of tales they had spun.

And yet, in truth, not all were gone.

Among the mortals walked any number of blessed – or cursed beings – however they chose to view it, with an ageless life. Filtering among the common folk almost like sages, telling the stories to keep them alive. Living in anticipation of moments such as these.

Perhaps they gathered. Drawn from their corners of the globe at the merest whiff in the wind that something was coming. That their way of life might rise to dominance again.

With a shudder and start, Evair awoke. Blinking into the darkness, the rich, sharp odor of gold flooded his nostrils as he heaved in his first conscious breath in ages. His crystalline dream of The Dragon Shrine rising from the depths swirled in his mind, calling to him a word that had been lost to his memory.

Rise.

The monument itself still lay entombed away from the eyes of mortal men, but the insistence of the vision called on Evair to rise. To break into the sun just as the Shrine had done and stand as a beacon on the soil.

Evair's heart thundered in his chest, louder than the clarion quake that thrust the symbol of his kind into the center of his dream. His body shook, and the heretofore dreamless slumber that had cocooned him cracked and fell away.

The ground so far above him lay still and untouched. The meadows still rolled in their peaceful acres, blissfully unaware of the reverie this sleeping Dragon had just visited upon them. The Dragon Shrine still lay buried, covetously hidden from the world.

Whether it had been a premonition or a mere dream was impossible for Evair to say. It was a fantasy, to be certain, but one of startling force. As if its foundations lay in a truth not yet written.

It was so clear, he told himself. His own voice sounded strange in the porches of his brain. Perhaps half a millennium had passed, and his joints creaked with disuse, and yet it had all seemed like the flapping of a butterfly wing. Years danced by faster than a child could tear the petals off a flower and count the wishes.

Air.

He needed to see the world again. Taste the sweet fragrance of the sea, and feel the sun bake his scales and warm his blood. He shifted, smiling to himself at the mass of treasure amassed around him. Cradling him in wealth as he slumbered.

Pushing against the weight of the earth, he arched his back, working his muscles until the ridge of his spine broke through the vale of coins and jewels. At last, that cool damp of the mother from whence we all come kissed his shoulders. The chill of it was sweeter than he could have remembered.

The hearty musk of it flooded his nostrils, and he breathed deeply. Forcing one of his talons up along the line of his body, he wedged it over his head, clawing away at the covering earth. Bit by bit, it yielded, and what was at first impenetrable soon received him like a lover.

It softened, and he began to dig. We think of digging as something we do toward the center of the Earth. Whether to plant a tree, or to bury treasure, or a loved one, each advancement is away from the air. But Evair was on a different trajectory. He burrowed toward the light like the mightiest of moles.

He was deep, but as he strove, he could feel the change. As he rose, it all became easier. Whether that was because he was becoming used to the labor or because the weight of ages was spilling away from him was hard to say. But, one thing was certain, the ground was growing warmer. And the warmth redoubled his strength.

All at once, he met that mass of roots from his dream. That meshed knot of vitality feeding the trees that stretched toward the sun. It seemed a crime to tear them, but the air was so close that he was maddened with it. That roar within his chest had become a siege, and his Dragon's heart was not to be denied.

Then, at last, a rush of fresh breath met his

nostrils. A peek of light shone through the murk, and he answered it with a herculean push. With a boundless sense of space and the deafening roar of the world, his head came into the light.

Squeezing his eyes shut against the blinding glare, he wriggled harder. His talons came to rest on the sun-drenched grass, and he dragged the whole of himself out of darkness and back into the realm of men. With a tremendous shake, he sent up a cloud of dust and dirt on every side, at last stretching his wings to feel the heat on their taut skin.

His whole body was one immense ache, and he indulged in extending each bit of himself to fight the twinge of each muscle. It was glorious.

Why haven't I done this sooner?

"I told you!" The voice broke over him, excited almost to frenzy. The light still stung his eyes, but he squinted to see who was celebrating. It was an old man in a wide brimmed hat. His clothes were strange to Evair, and he was gazing at him with an intent, almost unparalleled glee.

"Shut up, Fetterson!" Blinking again but growing more accustomed to the light, Evair saw another man. His chin was tucked low, and he bent his glare directly on the reawakened Dragon.

"Don't talk to me like that," Fetterson protested. "I brought you here. It's my research…"

"Research ain't shit. Not anymore. What matters is him." The younger man stabbed a finger at Evair. He was dressed in dark colors, with a mane of black hair pulled back loosely from his face. His sleeveless shirt revealed well muscled arms decked with tattoos and scars.

Even without an introduction, Evair knew his kind.

This was a Dragon slayer. They were all the same, and no passing of time could dull the familiar bloodlust and avarice in his eyes. Evair's hackles rose, and every fiber of him tensed in awful preparation.

"What about the agreement," Fetterson wailed.

"You'll be paid." The slayer began a slow circle of his quarry, growling, "just as soon as I claim this beast's lair."

"Sure of yourself, aren't you?" Evair's voice was full in his throat, presaging the whirlwind that lay dormant inside him. In response, the slayer merely smirked and continued his circle. The Dragon had seen that level of arrogant certainty many times in the past. And every face that wore it had fallen in battle.

All at once, The slayer leapt into action, dropping into a crouch and pulling a pair of silver blades from his boots. Springing into a charge, he made directly for Evair's underbelly, ready to plunge the searing silver into his heart.

He's a brave one.

Evair reared back to his full height, extending his wings and bringing them forward with a mighty snap. The wind of them forced the slayer to his knees and sent Fetterson sprawling in the grass like a child's toy.

"Don't be a fool, Walker," Fetterson puffed from the ground. "You can't do this alone."

"I've prepared my whole life for this," Walker sneered, getting back to his feet. "I'm not about to shame my family's name by engaging in anything other than single combat."

"Walker?" The name cut into Evair's core just as surely as one of those blades the slayer carried. The Walkers were a storied and ancient family whose lineage reached back almost as far as Evair's own kind. As the Dragon breathed the name, he saw a glint of terrible pride in his adversary's eyes.

"That's right, Dragon. Evair of the NetherVales, I've come for you."

"Then come for me!" Again, spreading wide, he

displayed himself to Walker's view, daring him to chance it all. The slayer took the bait and bolted across the grass, the fury of greed burning in his eyes. Rearing back, he raised one of those deadly blades, aiming directly at the center of Evair's chest.

With a lightning fast swipe, the Dragon lashed out a hand and scooped Walker into the air. In the shock of it, one of those knives tumbled to the ground, sticking firmly in the freshly upset soil.

"Hubris," Evair smiled. "Just like all of your kind."

"I could say the same." With that, Walker plunged his remaining knife into the back of Evair's hand. The silver immediately sent a sizzle through his blood, and the Dragon pealed out a horrible wail. His talons opened on reflex, and the slayer fell from a terrible height, crashing onto the ground with a thud.

He tried to rise, but something about him was broken. Perhaps his leg or his spine. It didn't matter to Evair. In a moment, the daring bastard would be dead. Plucking the blade from his hand, Evair turned hateful eyes on the fallen slayer.

"Do you know what justice is?" He advanced slowly. "Justice is sinking the weapon of your family line into your own heart. So that, whenever your story is written, it will be a warning to the rest of your line."

Something Evair had never seen before rushed up onto the green. It was a kind of chariot but enclosed and lacking the team to draw it. A door swung open from the side, and Fetterson leapt out, scrambling to collect the fallen Walker. Evair was so thunderstruck that he stood frozen in place.

"Come on," Fetterson grumbled as he struggled to raise his companion.

"No!" Foolhardy as slayers can be, Walker seemed intent on staying. "If I'm marked to die, it's my destiny."

"Don't be a fucking idiot," the older man snarled and dragged Walker bodily to this lightly rumbling chariot. Once stuffed inside, the door slammed shut, and it turned and tore off across the countryside.

Evair's confusion boiled over into rage. Not merely that he had lost the open opportunity for vengeance, but that he had felt compelled to return in the first place. The humans had always held a special enmity for Dragonkind, and the malice of it blistered the inside of the Dragon's chest.

Diving into the air like a bolt of lightning, he let

his wings carry him high until he could see the whole of the world splayed out under him like a fearful virgin. The world was full of humans. And Evair made a pact with himself as he soared through the sky.

Vengeance, he swore. *Every human who crosses my path shall perish.*

Looking at the gash on the back of his hand, he smeared the blood as if to bind his oath.

2
PENELOPE

Whisper Falls was the kind of town that lived up to its name. Things ambled along at an easy, almost lazy, pace, and it would have taken a significant shakeup for it to ascend to the level of 'quaint'. In truth, it sat nestled in a valley like a jewel in the landscape. The perfect refuge for those who wanted to live a life away from the hustle of the outside world.

Crash!

It was the fifth time Penelope Cloverlid had struggled to put a wooden chest of scrolls on the highest shelf of her apothecary shop. Each time she'd managed to avoid a catastrophe, but evidently, the fifth time wasn't the charm.

"Rats," she muttered to herself. If she'd been planning ahead, a charm might have been just the thing to lift the unwieldy little box into place.

Instead, she'd been stubborn, and now the scrolls were scattered all over the floor. As Penelope knelt to pick up the chest, she saw the fall had done some damage. A long crack was running through the wooden bottom.

"An ounce of prevention is worth a pound of cure." She sighed. It was what she always told her customers, even though few of them were inclined to listen. "Maybe you should try taking your own advice, Penny," she admonished herself.

Sitting on the floor and pulling the chest into her lap, Penelope began to murmur a few words. A casual listener might have thought they were nothing but nonsense. That casual listener would've been quite wrong. They were old Latin, which Penelope had long ago selected as her Language of Power.

The witch's index finger began to shine with the kind of light seen hovering over marshes in the middle of the night, except somehow, a little friendlier. She traced the tip of her finger along the crack, coaxing the wood of the chest to grow again, only for a moment. The rupture slowly began to close in the wake of her hand.

"There," she said, observing her work with satisfaction. The fix had been a small piece of magic, but Penelope tried to find enjoyment in everything she did. She found that helped keep her moving forward when it would have been so easy to succumb to the sadness lurking within her heart.

Shaking off the thought, she collected the scrolls, finding one all the way under her multi-tier display of herbal candles. Penelope considered using another insignificant charm to get it but decided she'd rather not waste the energy. She never knew when something big might come up and demand her full reserves.

Lore had come down through her family to be gentle with their powers. The Cloverlid women had a wealth of abilities latent inside them, but the family wisdom was to be careful of overtaxing them. Her grandmother had been a witch of prodigious power, and Penelope ached in her desire for that kind of scope.

To date, her specialty lay in smaller magicks. Healing. Minor spells.

She knew there had to be more dwelling somewhere within her, but she never chased her private light for fear of scaring it away. As if to question what abilities she had might be to wish them into nonexistence. And, she was fiercely covetous of what she possessed.

At times, when loneliness overtook her, she felt like it was all she had left of her family.

Wriggling forward on her belly, Penelope reached her arm under the bottom shelf. She was so close, her fingertips brushing the soft vellum.

The doorbell jingled and Penelope jerked, giving the display a hard bump. She heard rather than saw the candles wobbling. Immediately she spoke a quick spell and sat back up. Several columns of scented wax hovered in the air, frozen by her magic. One large three wick candle hung above precisely where her head would have been.

Not a wasted spell then, although so much for conserving her energy as much as possible.

"Goodness! Are you alright, Penny?" Violet Goldworthy stood in the middle of the shop, cocking her grey head. "What on earth are you doing on the floor? And *what* is going on with those candles?"

"Oh, nothing." Penelope stood up and dusted

herself off. She'd have to retrieve that pesky scroll later.

"Oooh, is it a spell?" The elderly woman's gaze grew avid. "May I watch?"

"It was merely a cantrip to prevent either my head or the candles splitting," explained Penelope, smiling fondly. Whisper Falls had never had a witch before, which made the townsfolk both extremely grateful for her work and extremely curious about her magic.

"Well! Speaking of head splitting, I hope you can spin me something similar," proclaimed Violet, her tone becoming a touch dramatic. "I have a terrible headache! It's been coming on every single day at 3 o'clock exactly, can you believe that?"

"That does sound terrible," soothed Penelope. "How many days has this been going on?"

"Today is the second," her patient announced, not self-conscious at all about the fact that two days didn't exactly make a trend. Penelope smothered a smile and turned to her herbal remedies.

"I'm glad you came in when you did." She pulled open the drawer bearing the handwritten label 'Headaches' in a tiny bronze frame. "What sort of headache is it?"

"An awful one!" Violet lowered herself onto the

velvet chaise lounge Penelope kept for waiting customers.

"Of course. But I mean, is it piercing pain? Dull throbbing pain? Pain behind your eye?"

"It's more like someone has wrapped a metal band around my entire head and is drawing it tighter and tighter," mused Violet. Then she sat up, a glint in her eye. "Do you think I could've been cursed?"

Penelope laughed and plucked a packet of herbs from the drawer.

"Nobody would ever want to curse you, Violet," she said, walking to the register. "You know you're one of the town favorites."

Violet blushed with pleasure.

"Oh, you're a sweetheart," she demurred, waving her hand. "Just like your father, full of flattery."

Despite herself, Penelope felt her face fall at the mention of her father. She knew she was like him in a million small ways, but that knowledge didn't bring her any comfort. It only made her miss him even more.

"I'm sorry, Penny dear." Violet looked at her searchingly. Whatever she saw on Penelope's face made her heave herself to her feet, looking genuinely contrite. "I didn't mean to upset you."

"I'm fine. He's been gone for a whole year. I'm used to it now." Penelope put the palm sized fabric bag on the counter. "So, what you'll…"

"You don't have to get use to it," interrupted Violet gently. "My Arnold died, oh, seven years ago now. I'll never stop missing him."

Swallowing the sob that rose in her throat, Penelope tried to shake off her grief.

"Thank you for the kind words," she replied, as cordially as she could. "But as I was saying, what you'll want to do with these is drink a cup of this tea whenever you feel a headache coming on. Two teaspoons of this mixture, steeped in eight ounces of water for fifteen minutes should do it."

"No spell?" Violet looked at her pleadingly, and Penelope was relieved the older woman had been distracted away from the conversation about her father's death.

"There's some magic in those herbs already," explained Penelope. "And besides, you know I don't do magic on customers unless it's an emergency. If I did, I'd run out of energy by lunchtime!"

That wasn't precisely true. Penelope was a very powerful witch, but it was in her best interests if the townspeople didn't know that. Life was much easier if everyone thought the most she could do was help a broken bone heal straight. She didn't want wealthy people coming from far away, trying to bribe massive magical workings out of her.

"Yes yes, I know. And if you say this cure will do the trick, then I know it will." Violet dug around in her purse for what she always called her billfold. "*And* I love tea. Although, my favorite mug shattered this past Sunday." She clucked and shook her head. "It was too close to the edge of the shelf when that tremor rolled through."

"Oh no!" Penelope seized on the new subject happily. "Those tremors have really been something, haven't they? I had to change a bunch of displays in the shop, so everything breakable was secured."

"They're very unnerving." Violet placed a few bills in Penelope's outstretched hand. "We've never had anything like them, and I've lived here for fifty years."

"I know. I looked it up on the internet," Penelope agreed. "This area is supposed to be too tectonically stable for anything like what we've been experiencing recently."

"The internet," grumbled Violet. "I don't know

what you need to consult a bunch of anonymous gossips writing on the websites to know what any local could tell you. These tremors aren't normal."

"It must be the sleeping Dragons under the mountain waking up," joked Penelope, to hide her giggle at Violet's characterization of the internet.

"Shhh!" Violet grew suddenly serious. She leaned forward and grabbed Penelope's wrist. Her bony fingers were stronger than they looked. "Don't say such things, not out loud."

"It's only a myth." Puzzled, Penelope tugged her wrist out of Violet's grip so she could make change.

"All myths are rooted in reality." There wasn't a hint of the drama Penelope expected in Violet's voice. "So let's not tempt fate."

"Okay," said Penelope, raising her eyebrow. She handed Violet a tumble of coins. "I'll just stick with complaining about the tremors, I guess."

"See that you do." Violet sighed, putting away her change. That done, she straightened, some of her playful energy returning. "Now I'm off to brew a cup of this right away. You take care of yourself, Penelope dear. Make sure you eat enough! Angelica's Bakery is right across the street, for goodness's sake!"

With one last pleasant exchange about cookies and pies, Penelope saw her customer out. She watched for a few seconds as the older woman shuffled down Main Street. Penelope was surprised to find Violet so superstitious but not in the least affected by her concerns.

The witch shrugged, turning back to her shop. There were plenty of stories about Dragons and their hoards, but no one had seen so much as a wing of a Dragon in centuries. They had probably all died out hundreds of years ago.

"Died out?" Penelope chuckled, scoffing at herself. Even that idea was a fantasy.

Most likely, Dragons had never existed in the first place.

3
EVAIR

Clouds scudded across the sky like huge smears of white paint on the canvas of the blue sky. The sun shone, glinting off riverways and lakes below, and the birds sang. Until, that is, a massive shadow passed over them, and they fell silent

Evair swooped and dove between those pale fluffed behemoths in the sky, emerging from cover only long enough to examine the world beneath him, then returning. His pearlescent scales were the perfect camouflage amidst the clouds, except when the sun caught him at just the right angle, and he glistened like a jewel in his hoard.

Dragons traditionally avoided the eyes of men. Too many times, a greedy mortal had pursued a

Dragon to the ground for nothing more than a goblet of gold. Year after year, humans shrieked their terror when a Dragon chose to lair even so much as ten miles from them. Evair knew that to maintain this tradition would be best, but his heart still boiled with rage.

Rage... and confusion. The mountain range he had chosen for his rest was not the same as when he went to sleep. For a radius of many miles around his place of slumber, certainly, the forests were as wild, the meadows as green, and the stone as jagged as he remembered. Yet as he flew towards the edge of the range, he saw newness. Things that shouldn't be there.

Threading from a valley between two peaks, a long black ribbon traveled over the shoulders of the mountains. Spotting glistening dots moving far below, Evair had to assume the black curving path was a road, albeit made of some material he couldn't identify from the sky. Although the dots were too polished and too fast to be the carriages he remembered, the movement made their purpose clear. Perhaps they were more fiendish human inventions, like the cursed chariot that had stolen Walker from his vengeance.

The stripped swath of forest, a bald patch on

the luscious fur of the Earth, was definitely the result of human interference. A mine, if Evair did not miss his guess. A gust of renewed anger escaped his maw, and the power of his Windstorm breath shredded a tuft of cloud to pieces.

How dared the humans mine the range Evair had chosen as his own? The Dragon understood the desire to acquire wealth. After all, he had it himself in spades. To purge a landscape of all living things, though... that he could not condone.

Evair convulsed with wrath, writhing in the air. The wound on his hand tore as he did so, sending massive droplets of crimson blood to earth like some macabre rain. He ignored the pain, looking only for some way to vent his spleen and fulfill his pact to himself.

There. His keen eyes caught the spires and rooftops of a human settlement nestled into the side of the mountain. It was small, but it would suit Evair's purpose well enough. He could demolish this town within minutes and move on. Perhaps he would pause his search for vengeance after this in favor of catching some fresh prey.

Evair's stomach echoed its support of this idea, but like his still dripping blood, the Dragon ignored it. Meat would not satiate him in the way his furious heart needed. Besides, if he were lucky, a human would wander away in the chaos Evair was about to cause. Then Evair's teeth could sink into human flesh without anyone the wiser.

He banked, his huge wings catching the sun and pulling him to an abrupt stop over the settlement. Low hanging fog hovered above the wooded slopes backing the town. Evair grinned a Dragon's grin, full of sharp teeth and menace. That fog was the world's gift to him, offering the perfect hiding place from which to watch his revenge.

He shot high into the air and began to breathe. Twisting his body, he wound round and round, whipping a violent wind into being. As he twisted, he fell, exhaling all the while, until a newly born and vicious column of a tornado began to barrel away from him.

Diving at the edges of the tornado he'd made, Evair sent out a few more blasts in the direction of the settlement for good measure. Caught by the strength of his Breath Weapon, the roof of the nearest building ripped off to tumble away, cascading into other human structures. Shingles flapped away on the wind like sharp birds, striking a nearby human on the forehead.

Snorting with pleasure, Evair watched as his

tornado bit into the black line of road leading into the center of the mortal town. More humans threw themselves out of their gleaming horseless chariots, running for cover. Some frantically tried to secure what looked like storefronts, while others scooped children into their arms, hunching over their charges.

Flowers were ripped out of window boxes, and the brittle sound of splintering filled the air. Doors rattled like they would fly clean off their hinges. A glass window shattered as a bulky wooden shutter smashed into it, sending shards cascading over the sidewalk.

Yet, Evair's creation was not allowed to do this fierce work for long. Out of the corner of his gaze, Evair saw a flash of red-gold hair, as eye catching as any precious metal beaten to a brilliant sheen. He turned.

A witch stood in the path of the tornado, feet planted and hands glowing. Her locks snapped with the terrible wind, but she did not give way. White throat moving as she shouted words Evair knew to be arcane, the witch faced down his windstorm.

Those luminous hands tore at nothing in front of her, and pieces of the tornado were peeled away like loose skin. The winds slowed, going from a roiling mass of gusts to a coiling column of breezes. With one last elegant gesture, the witch brought the whole thing to a complete halt.

Evair gaped, shocked at the speed at which his creation was reduced to nothing. The skeleton of the tornado hovered for a few seconds, trembling, and then collapsed, sending dust exploding outwards.

Without the tornado between them, there was nothing to keep the witch from seeing Evair. He had a few seconds of grace as she coughed and shook her head, trying to wipe the debris from her face.

A new rage filled Evair's veins at the failure of his mission. He wanted nothing but to eat this strange witch who had foiled his plans. However, he was no longer a young Dragon, and in such a dire situation, not even great anger could override his hard earned wisdom. The mortals must not know of his existence, no matter what.

In an attempt to hide, Evair turned to flee into the shielding embrace of the fog. He beat his wings, trying for speed, but to his confusion, speed would not come. It felt as though he was dragging his wings through mud instead of air.

Swallowing a roar of frustration, he tensed all his muscles, trying to surge forward with his whole body. An acidic bolt of pain shot through him, and instead of moving towards the fog, he dropped lower.

His wound had opened from a slice into a gash. Red blood welled from it, splashing down to the earth below. Evair blinked, unable to comprehend what he saw. The fog had moved from the mountainside into his mind, and he couldn't think clearly.

The moment of bewilderment cost him. A true wind, created by no mythic beast but by the forces of Earth herself, was rushing down the mountain. It rustled the treetops and tore leaves from branches, and then it caught Evair, his wingspan fully extended. With the inexorable apathy of nature, the wind threw him hard to the ground.

He crashed into the dirt, sending sprays of brown flying. His head hit something hard, a large rock embedded in the soil. His vision blurred with the blow to his temple as a rusty puddle of mud dampened by his blood spread out from his wounded limb.

A shape came nearer to him, tall and slender. Evair struggled to focus as the dust cleared.

Another step and the shape revealed itself as the witch, her red hair curling around her face and her green eyes flashing.

Evair raised one scythe like claw in warning but knew it was futile. He'd seen enough of her battle with the tornado to know this witch had power. She'd seen enough of his presence behind the tornado to know it was his doing. He'd hurt her fellow mortals, and no matter how many times those fellow mortals had hurt him, she would still believe revenge was her right.

She would kill him.

Never one to go down without a fight, Evair tried one last time to summon a breath of windstorm from his throat. Nothing escaped but a tremulous cough, like he was nothing but a Dragon kit learning how to use his Breath Weapon for the first time.

Shame and misery washed away the remnants of anger in Evair's veins. He'd lived so long, only for this to be his end?

He met the witch's eyes, surprised to find himself drawn into their emerald depths. For an instant, he felt the strangest feeling. It was like he'd come home at last and would yearn no more.

No sooner had he registered this feeling than

he rejected it as nonsense, mere twinges from an exhausted mind. The injustice of his plight burned away any bit of that odd contented calm, right as a black curtain began to shroud his gaze.

The witch took a step closer, finally in range for the killing blow he knew to be coming. The last thing he saw was that she lifted a glowing hand before the darkness rose up and claimed him.

4
PENELOPE

Penelope gaped at the huge, scaled, and very much real Dragon lying at her feet. It turned out that not only did Dragons exist in general, but they also existed right now, directly in front of her.

The mythic beast wasn't moving. Its wings sprawled lifeless in the dirt, and its horned head lay on its side, eyes closed. Closest to Penelope, one pearl white forearm extended, dagger like claws digging into the dirt. A wound oozed on that forearm, a gash that traveled down to a deep gouge in the Dragon's hand. Red black blood fell in slow, viscous drops to the ground, forming a pool that soaked into the earth.

Penelope stood frozen despite the Dragon's

motionlessness. Shock and fear were lacing through her bones. That tornado must have been this Dragon's creation. There was no other explanation except for coincidence, and Penelope didn't believe in dismissing logic in favor of coincidence.

One, after months of tremors, a Dragon had appeared for the first time in centuries. Penelope would bet her entire stock of charmed crystals that it was the one said to have slumbered under the mountain. Violet had been right. Myths were rooted in reality.

Two, Whisper Falls wasn't the kind of place that had tornados. Scientifically, Penelope knew that the rough mountain landscape shouldn't allow them to form, and anecdotally, she'd never heard of one going through the area. Her father would have mentioned it, especially given how much damage this one had caused in less than a minute.

No, it was impossible to believe that a tornado and the appearance of this Dragon were unrelated. Yet that begged the question: why on earth would this Dragon want to attack Whisper Falls?

In the time it took for all of this to rush through Penelope's mind, the Dragon still did not so much as twitch. The witch knelt, her initial terror dissipating at the thought that he might be dead.

He? Penelope paused in the motion of reaching her hand towards the Dragon's scaly hide. How was she suddenly sure that the Dragon was male? And for that matter, why should she care about the beast? After all, he'd threatened her home and her neighbors, and she wasn't sure that even her power could defeat him in full battle mode.

Penelope didn't know why she felt the way she did, but she couldn't deny that she did not wish for the death of this Dragon. It seemed wrong that such an impressive and legendary creature should perish for seemingly no reason. That idea might be overly romantic silliness, but whether it was or it wasn't, she could find out with one simple spell.

Murmuring in Latin under her breath, Penelope raised her hands. They were luminescent once more, but this time, instead of the glow collecting around her fingers, a small pool of light grew between her palms. When it was perhaps the size of a dessert plate, she tossed it gently into the air.

The radiant circle drifted down to hover over the Dragon's pearly back. Penelope took a few deep breaths. Slowly, the white luminescence began to turn blue. It was the blue of life; the sky reflected in deep, pure water.

This Dragon was not an evil Dragon.

Penelope sat back on her heels, staring in wonder. The spell she'd just cast was a favorite of hers, as it tested the general will of living beings. Not a single action or a particular motivation, but the being's moral inclination. If the Dragon had been evil, the pool of light would've turned an oily black.

Instead, it turned blue, and the question of why the Dragon would attack Whisper Falls became even more puzzling.

Penelope pushed her curiosity aside. In that instant, it didn't matter why the Dragon had chosen to do what he'd done. It only mattered that he was hurt and didn't deserve to be.

Scooting to hover over his wounded hand, she began to intone the words of a generalized healing spell. A little web of light spun itself between her fingers. With a flick of her wrists, Penelope sent it to land on the Dragon's shoulders. When it touched him, the web grew over his scales, curving lines of moonlight soon covering his hide.

Closing her eyes, Penelope still saw the web, and beneath it, an indescribable impression of the

Dragon's health. With the help of her spell, the knowledge entered Penelope's mind that there was a poison in the Dragon's blood.

She nodded to herself, beginning to understand one thing at least. Poison was the answer to how such a small wound could bring down such a powerful creature. Keeping herself focused, she began to use her magic to burn away the toxin. Chasing it through her massive patient's veins, she eliminated it swiftly and completely.

It was almost like the Dragon's body itself was helping the witch. She'd never been able to counter a poison so quickly, not to mention that she'd never had a patient the size of two or three horses.

The same thing happened when Penelope released the web, letting it sink into the Dragon's skin. The spell, once absorbed, would lend its strength towards knitting together any flesh wounds, speeding up the natural healing process slightly. As she watched, though, there was nothing slight about the speed at which the Dragon's gash closed up.

One moment, it was trickling blood into a pool beneath his forearm. The next, his scales were smooth and uninterrupted, not even a scar where the injury had been. Penelope's eyes widened. She thought it must be the Dragon's metabolism that worked such a wonder. Magical creatures often burned so much energy by merely existing.

Even with an explanation in her mind, Penelope couldn't stop herself from reaching out and touching the place where the Dragon no longer bled. It was a miracle, seeing such a laceration disappear so fast. Her forefinger encountered unbroken hide, covered in polished and sleek scales for the barest second. Then, she was touching skin.

Penelope jerked back, her mouth falling open. In front of her very eyes, the Dragon had shifted. Wings were narrowing, claws softening, body shrinking, the beast had become… a human.

A very, *very* attractive, and very, *very* naked, human.

Where the Dragon had lain, there sprawled seven feet of nude male muscle. Powerful legs traveled up to a sculpted backside and narrow hips, which broadened to a brawny chest and corded shoulders.

The once triangular head was now rounded, with soft white hair waving over his temples. Those jaws that could so easily have snapped her leg in half had become a strong, masculine jawline framing soft kissable lips.

Penelope sucked in a breath and clasped her hands against her chest. What was she doing, thinking that this Dragon man had a kissable mouth? Clearly, she was overwhelmed by the wonder of his transformation, and her brain was attempting to render the situation a more familiar one.

It was unfortunate for her mind then that this situation was undoubtedly far beyond unusual, perhaps landing all the way at unimaginable. An injured Dragon had collapsed to the earth inches from Penelope, and shortly after she healed him, he turned into a gorgeous, if still entirely unconscious, human man.

The witch's keen ears caught stirrings behind her. All the townspeople had gone for cover when the tornado appeared, but it had been many minutes since Penelope tore it apart. The folks of Whisper Falls were beginning to emerge, which meant she had to move.

Part-time human or not, if the locals found out a Dragon was the reason their beloved home had been put in danger, they'd kill him. Hell, if they knew he'd attacked them, they'd probably take advantage of his vulnerable human form and lynch him then and there.

Penelope quickly cast an invisibility spell. She felt a lurch of nausea as it took hold, signaling to her that she'd overdone it magically already. It turned out she'd been right after all to attempt to conserve her energy instead of doing many little charms to make her life easier.

Yet she'd have to find the reserves to cast one more spell if she had any hope of getting this hunk of a man back to her house. It was risky, but it was the only option for him to recover safely.

Taking a deep breath, Penelope began to murmur once more. Her voice caught in her throat, the words resisting her. Her magic was nearly tapped out, but something pushed her forward. With one last croaky syllable, she pushed a seed of light out from her palm and into the man's bare chest.

For an instant, Penelope thought she might throw up. The nausea had become more than a twinge, but she managed to steady herself. The invisibility spell she'd cast wouldn't be very effective if the townspeople now milling around the street saw vomit emerge from thin air.

Once her stomach had settled as much as it

could, Penelope slid her arm under the man's back. She tugged his arm over her shoulders with her free hand and pulled him up to a limp sit with no effort. Her spell had worked despite its painful casting, and her charge currently weighed a fifth of his true weight.

Dragging the man up so that he was draped over her smaller frame, Penelope began to inch back to her house. Avoiding the townspeople took a little effort, but soon enough, she'd turned off of Main Street and was making her way to the cozy cottage that she called home.

She expected to feel relief once she'd closed the door behind her, but instead, a new sensation took hold of her. It wasn't fear, precisely, although it wasn't unrelated. It was more of a prickling astonishment at her own actions. Standing there in her entryway, she finally realized what she'd done.

She'd brought a Dragon home with her.

5
EVAIR

For the second time in barely two days, Evair stirred from a deep, heavy slumber. His consciousness returned to him slowly, sleep laying on him as heavy as the many feet of earth he'd rested beneath for centuries.

He was no longer ensconced in soil, however. As Evair began to awaken more truly, he felt his limbs cradled in an unexpectedly soft substance. The Dragon blinked leaden eyelids open to find no bower of earth surrounded him, but rather a strange and squishy bed.

The torpor fell from his eyes more swiftly at that. Confused at being stranded on his back, Evair attempted to right himself. He dug his elbow into the cushioned surface, pushing hard for purchase.

The motion sent a twinge through his hand, and he hissed, dropping back into the softness beneath his head.

A memory of a Dragon slayer and a silver knife plunged into his flesh sprang into his head. Yes, that was right, he'd been wounded by a treacherous snake of a human. That twinge, though... it hadn't been the pain of an open gash. It was more the ache of an injury newly healed, warning one's body to not demand too much too soon.

Evair brought his forearm up reflexively to check the site of his wound. The sight that met his eyes brought him surging up to sitting, growling with disbelief.

He was in his human guise. Vulnerable and thin skinned, wearing the yielding flesh of a human rather than the scaled armor of a Dragon.

Immediately, Evair tried to shift back to his mightier self, to no effect. The hand within his field of vision stayed long flexible fingers rather than sharp claws. He remained wingless, tailless, too small.

A howl of frustration and confusion escaped Evair's throat. New memories assailed him of a human settlement on a mountainside and an unknown witch shredding his windstorm to pieces of harmless breeze. He had been in battle, then... so why in the ancestor's name would he have reduced himself to his puny human shape?

Evair had not been human for a long time, since decades before he lay himself down to rest. The shape of his body was foreign to him. Was this the human guise he'd always had? He could barely remember willingly putting himself in this soft, malleable skin, even at times of complete peace. Why would Evair give up his claws, his teeth?

Something was wrong. As the fog of sleep had fully cleared from his mind, Evair knew this with complete certainty. He was a prisoner in his skin, trapped in a form that reduced him to a shadow of his true power.

Walker. That Dragon slayer who'd escaped the death he deserved. He must have done something to Evair. The bastard must have some horrible plan that involved Evair in his human form. Why else would he have worked this magic and not killed his Dragon prey?

The unbidden thought of Walker considering him prey sent a surge of rage through Evair. Instinctively, he tried to shift again. Nothing.

"Coward!" Evair bellowed his fury, twisting around to look at every corner of the small room.

It resembled no prison he had ever seen before, well appointed with furnishings and a few elegant trinkets. This made no sense.

What knavery had brought him to this place? What game was Walker playing? He had restrained Evair magically, yet not physically, showing a hubris that would not stand. By trapping Evair in human form, the vile Dragon slayer had committed a worse violation than simple murder.

Perhaps the knave imagined he could torture Evair. Perhaps Walker and the witch were working together and would try to use Evair's flesh and blood and bone for their wicked spells. Perhaps they thought they could force Evair to give up the resting places of other Dragons, all in hopes of killing his kind in their sleep, defenseless.

Evair roared again, the sound small and pathetic as it came from his human throat. What kind of craven weakling would reduce his foe through tricks and subterfuge? The name of Walker already dripped with evil savagery, but this! This indignity brought a new level of gutless depravity to that hated family's reputation.

His ears were still keener than those of mortals, despite this form's aggravating limitations, and Evair heard footsteps from beyond the room rushing towards him. An image presented itself in his mind: Walker, gloating and taunting him while he remained trapped in this feeble shape.

That did it. The idea of his enemy having such control finally built to a peak. As Evair screamed his ferocious ire, he suddenly transformed. He hadn't reached for the shift intentionally, but the anger coursing through his veins left scales in its wake.

As the Dragon's body manifested, his bulk burst into being in a space not intended for it. There was a cracking sound as the ceiling caved in over his arched spine and a crumbling sound as his wings knocked the plaster walls apart. Dust rose around him as he reared, victorious and ready to face the evil Walker.

"What in the name of the seven circles of hell do you think you're doing?"

A human flung open the door, but it wasn't the Dragon slayer. Instead, it was a woman – a witch, if the sniff of power around her was any indication. Was it the same witch as the one who had destroyed Evair's tornado? The air was too thick with dust for him to be sure.

He breathed, and a cloud dissipated, enough for the Dragon to get a glimpse of the witch's face.

Merely that flash was enough to impress upon him that her eyes betrayed no fear but instead were filled with exasperated anger.

"Why would you shift back, confined within four walls? Don't you have an ounce of sense, or did that all get knocked out when you bit the dust earlier? Anyone with an eye to see could tell my house was not intended to hold hulking mythic beasts!"

The witch stood in silhouette with her hands on her hips, defiance and righteousness written all over her stance. Evair snapped his teeth ominously, but rather than run away screaming as she ought to, the witch stood her ground.

"Stop trying to be all intimidating you big brute," she insisted. "Shift back right now before you do any other damage!"

How dare this little woman command him to return to a worthless form? Was it her magic that had bound him? Evair opened his mouth, ready to eat the mouthy human. It was the fate that awaited all humans that challenged him, punishment for their foolishness and the return of peace and quiet.

Yet, a new and strange feeling was winding around Evair's heart. His open maw hovered mere feet from the witch, but something held him back.

He could not bring himself to close his jaws around her, despite the fact that she continued to yell at him. Her words receded into background noise as Evair hesitated. Floating through his head was the shimmering sense that she... *mattered.*

A human? Matter? Evair closed his mouth and sat back on his haunches, staring at the witch. Enough powdery particles had fallen to the ground that he could now make out her red hair. The tumbling locks sparked recognition in him, and he cast his mind back to the moment his tornado had been thwarted. This was the witch who had ruined his plans of vengeance.

For that alone, he ought to eat her. The disrespect to the workings of his Windstorm Breath could not stand, except... That strange feeling twined deeper into Evair's chest, sliding into his very blood.

As heat crept after the feeling, suffusing the Dragon's frame with a warmth that seared as much as it soothed, a realization crashed into Evair's mind.

This human female was his mate.

It was the only explanation for the sensations coursing through him. What else could so viscerally prevent him from silencing someone who would normally have considered an annoyance? The way his body responded to her was new to him, of course, but nonetheless, Evair simply knew.

He gazed down, seeing that the witch had come closer to him while he'd distractedly contemplated the stirrings of the mating bond. She was too near for comfort. He'd never let a human penetrate the radius of his wings, and yet her presence felt not at all threatening.

That is... until she reached out a hand and touched him.

Evair had a moment to experience the shockwave of pleasure and rightness that surged through him at her touch. Her fingers were soft against his scales, her palm warm. For an instant, he fancied he could feel her pulse through her hand, pumping through her heart and into his own chest.

Then, he was shifting again. The enjoyment of the physical connection to his mate was gone, chased away by startled resentment. His powerful scaled torso shrunk away from her hand, the feeling of her touch lost as his shoulders became rounded and his abdomen flattened.

"No!" The cry was torn from his throat, and the

sound of his own voice, so frail in comparison to the boom of his Dragon speech, brought home to him that he was trapped. Once again, his soul hammered at the cage of human flesh.

"What have you done to me?" He growled, limbs trembling with fury and overwhelming uncertainty. "What have you done?"

All thoughts of the mating bond had fled. Instead of reaching back out to the female whose presence resonated so profoundly with him, Evair crouched, getting into a battle stance. His every muscle tensed, his fingers curling into fists and his breath coming hard and fast.

If this witch thought she'd gotten herself a captive Dragon, she was in for a great surprise.

6
PENELOPE

Once again, Penelope found herself gaping in surprise and wonder. And, it must be said, a little irritation, too. The destruction to the room was substantial, and she would have to plan very carefully how best to address it. A combination of magic and good old-fashioned elbow grease was likely.

But, more than that, Penelope wrestled with an overarching feeling of connection. Connection to a creature that was so hostile and destructive created such a battle in her mind. Was there a world in which this man/Dragon (who was so clearly at odds with those around him) could elicit such a strong bond with just a touch?

Penelope shook her head. It was obvious she

was living in that world at this precise moment, and these conflicting feelings of fear, awe, attachment, and wonder would need some deep unpacking.

But now was not the time. Penelope ordered the sparks that flew within her chest to recede and stand down with a stern inner command. She needed all her powers of discernment, logic, and negotiation with her now. She surmised it would take a plethora of tactics to get a firm handle on the situation.

Her strange feelings of magnetism towards this mysterious creature would have to wait.

Turning back to the immediate situation in front of her, Penelope had to have a stern conversation with her eyeballs. Specifically, where they needed to be directed. For the man/Dragon, now fully in his human male form, was still wildly and vociferously naked. Every muscle rippled and seemed to deposit gobs of electricity into the surrounding air.

It was hard to know where to look. He did not seem shy or aware that his nakedness was discomfiting. Indeed, such nakedness actually provided him with the most power in the room. Penelope was acutely aware of this and ordered her gaze to fall somewhere squarely in the middle of his finely shaped forehead.

Drywall, pillow stuffing and debris surrounded him, his arms at his side poised to attack. Breath flared out of his nostrils, and his stance of legs wide apart suggested he was ready to pounce once more.

Hands raised, Penelope approached with caution. She moved slowly and carefully, not only to avoid any sudden surprises but also to avoid glass.

"Easy. Easy now. Alright. I may have overreacted before. Let's try this again." She kept her voice even and slow.

In response, he simply stared, his eyes tracking every minute movement. But Penelope thought she detected that his breathing began to slow. A good sign.

"I am Penelope. I am not here to hurt or imprison you. Merely wishing to help a fellow creature. Do you believe me?"

"If I'm not a prisoner, why am I here? What is this puny human shell?" He plucked at his skin, pinching it hard enough for Penelope to see it come away angry and red. A small part of her twinged at the sight of his flesh being handled in this way... even if it was by its very owner.

"That is a question I have myself. But it appears you have shapeshifting powers. I would venture to guess it's quite the survival technique. You can't argue it makes life easier when dealing with humans."

Even as Penelope said this, she knew she was only half right. Certainly, on the scale of being in a human world, going about as a full-fledged Dragon would be highly problematic. But there was no way this man would ever be able to hide in a crowd. His sheer height, shock of white hair, and unnamable magnetism would ensure he stood out no matter what.

Still, beggars can't be choosers.

"Why would I *ever* wish to deal with such a middling race? What have they to offer me that would be worth being in this limiting form?"

He continued to pluck, pick and generally snub each part of himself. Once again, Penelope stifled an urge to stay his hand and place her own hand on each angry welt.

"I wish I could tell you. But I do know that if the rest of the village saw your true form, you would be in quite a pickle. And while your human form is... formidable, I suggest we make the most of it."

"I am not intimidated by a rabble of worthless, pitch-forked humans," he growled, his hands clenching.

"And I'm in no way suggesting you should be. I am merely suggesting we try to find a way to ensure you are not fighting each and every moment of your day. That wound I found on you was not insignificant. Are you telling me you wish to spend every day like that?"

In an effort to reduce the temperature in the room, Penelope took a seat on the corner of her bed. Ideally, by making a show of a more casual way of engaging, she might allay his fight or flight instincts. Perhaps, she reasoned, this could become a conversation and not a hostage situation.

At this, he looked to his arm and connected her words to the now healed area. To Penelope's relief, it had the welcome effect of calming him further. She saw his shoulders release a little and his fighting stance lessen.

"Perhaps. I was unaware you are responsible for aiding my healing. I am grateful."

"My pleasure. I do what I can. Now, may I suggest we make you more, well, comfortable isn't the word, but perhaps more... G-rated?" Again, Penelope exerted an iron will to keep her eyes locked in the region of his face and not anywhere else.

"Whatever do you mean?" A hint of distrust crept into his voice.

"Perhaps getting you clothed would be a start. I don't have much that might fit, but it will do until we can figure out something more suitable."

He grunted as he looked back down again at his human form. Penelope noticed that goosebumps had appeared on his skin. Was he cold?

"What is your name? I owe you the pleasure of thanking you for healing me?" His voice softened, and Penelope was reminded of the blue light that hovered over him when she cast her spell of will, showing him to be a creature of good.

"Penelope. My name is Penelope. It is a pleasure to meet you."

"Ah, yes. A name that resounds with humans and has done so for many years. I am Evair."

Evair. Penelope rolled the name around in the fissures of her head like a marble. A shiny, *blue* marble.

"It is a sincere pleasure to meet you, Evair,"

Penelope intoned, enjoying the sensation of his name dancing off her tongue.

The tension in the room had somewhat dissipated, and Penelope took the opportunity it afforded to guide Evair into the adjacent room where a closet she had not opened in some time waited.

Taking a small breath in fortification, she opened its doors. Instantly, a familiar scent wafted up to her, causing her to momentarily start, instantly awash in memories. A flood of grief threatened to overwhelm her, but Evair's hesitant steps behind her brought her back to the here and now.

Selecting a dress shirt, some pants and various other items, she managed to cobble together an outfit that, while not necessarily perfect, was adequate. Evair's height made the pants resemble shorts, but she was pleased to find items that would accommodate his ample musculature.

Awkwardly, Evair dressed himself, snorting in frustration at the fiddly buttons and zips. After a quick assessment, Penelope decided they would have to find different clothing for him, but at least now he was covered, and her eyes could finally abate their almost obsessive lockdown on his forehead.

"That will have to do for now. How do you feel?" She stepped back to take in the whole effect.

His raw beauty and power had been somewhat diminished by her father's clothes, but as she looked him over, she recalled the last time she saw her father wearing that shirt, wearing that sweater. Breath caught in her throat, and she was forced to turn away from him.

"While I feel this clothing is beneath my station, it is certainly welcome. But I see I have done nothing but create a comical situation for you. Are you alright? You seem overcome by something." He stepped forward, his feet shuffling on the floor. The pants did not even come to his mid-calf.

Penelope had to recover quickly and made a zealous effort to do so, possibly overdoing it in the process.

"It is nothing. That closet has not been opened in some time. The dust is getting to me, that's all." She flicked her hand casually as if to emphasize her point.

Evair's eyes dipped as if he was assessing the veracity of her answer. It seemed he was not quite convinced, but he let the matter drop.

"I see. Yes. But they are most welcome. Thank you."

"Of course. Now, I am no expert on... what creatures such as you require, but it would seem to me that food would be in order. Yes?" Penelope wanted out of this room and an excuse to busy herself. Finding food was a worthy and easily justifiable task.

"Come to think of it, yes. I would like something to eat. I did not realize how famished I was." Evair rubbed his belly as if double-checking his human organs were sending him the correct signals.

"Right. Well, let's clean up a little here and find something for you. With the added bonus of exploring the human world... in a much safer way."

Evair became suspicious again, eyeing her narrowly.

"So, you admit that this world is unsafe for me. Then why take me out into it?" At that exact moment, his stomach rumbled. His hunger, now acknowledged, was becoming urgent.

"If we are going to do anything about that," she said, pointing to his stomach, "we are going to have to go out. But, whatever you might expect when we step out onto the street, I can assure you that things have changed a lot. You're going to have to find new ways of handling yourself."

"New ways?" His voice was guarded but softer than the near accusation of his former tone.

"Yep. I am willing to bet that you are going to find a lot of what you see confusing. If you can trust me, even a little, I will do what I can to help. But, I can tell you now that you will not do anyone any favors if you fly into a destructive spat again. Yes?"

"I understand you."

There was bound to be more explaining to do, but until Penelope was able to fully gauge the extent of his removal from the modern world, this little exchange would have to do. After all, the best plan might be to just explain along the way.

With a nod, Penelope returned to the ruined bedroom. While she did not wish to exert many magical powers, she could not leave it in this state. Just the bare minimum would do.

Bowing her head, she recited words in the spidery Latin that lay nestled in several drawers of her brain.

Within moments, streaks of light, buttery in color, eased from her hands, gentle and meandering. She lifted her head and directed the streaks around various parts of the room. At their touch, the ruined parts of the room began to reassemble themselves and return to their former locations.

Slabs of drywall, flecks of paint, and shards of glass rose and rebuilt themselves, traveling through the air as if floating down a lazy river. Within moments, the room more or less resembled what it had before.

Opening her eyes, Penelope looked about. Some paint and some rearranging would be necessary, but that could wait.

Evair stood in the doorway, impressed but doing his best to hide it. Turning to him, she sighed, and the last of the yellow streaks floated away.

"Alright. Let's get you fed."

7

EVAIR

"**Careful!**" Penelope's tiny hand caught Evair by the back of his shirt and pulled him up short just in time to see one of those chariots sail past.

"Watch the fuck out, asshole!" A red, furious face glared from the portal as the contraption roared by, leaving Evair far more nonplussed than angry. He turned and looked down at the woman who had effectively pulled him out of danger.

"You are going to have to look both ways before crossing. They don't really slow down."

I see.

Evair's reintroduction into the modern world was bewildering at first. Despite his deep belief that humans were a species of animal with limited and finite abilities, he could not deny the astonishing technological advances they had made since he had entered into his long hibernation.

After dodging the speeding chariot, they continued their walk into Whisper Falls proper. Penelope took on the role of tour guide with aplomb and patience, especially since Evair took some minutes to regain confidence walking as a biped again. The distribution of his body weight was entirely different, and several stumbles and near falls took place before he walked with confidence.

The village of Whisper Falls unrolled before them as they walked. Evair already knew what it looked like from afar. To his Dragon sight, it was merely a collection of puny human dwellings and places of business. A place he could meddle with as a child might with a wooden toy soldier.

Now, as a human himself, Evair experienced the village differently, and his mind reluctantly endeavored to see it through human eyes. The trouble with that was how startlingly different it all seemed.

Every time a new volley of vehicles careened past him, or some puny human nearly bumped into him while gazing at a small shining rectangle in their hand, it only frustrated him more. As if the whole of the world was bent as one specifically to intrude upon his peace.

"Trust me," Penelope said, just managing to distract Evair from sending an offending pedestrian sprawling to the pavement. "It may not seem like it now, but you are going to want one of those things."

"Never," he sniffed. "Whatever those terrible things are, if they reduce your kind to such mindless, inattentive cretins, I want nothing to do with them."

"Well, I've got one, and I like to think I'm not a cretin," she said with a small smile. "It's all in how you engage with them."

"Perhaps." Small cinders of rage burned at the edges of his mind, but he was compelled by Penelope's reasoning. It was in his best interest to seek food, seek comfort, and seek security in human form. At least for now.

Now that his head was clearer and his wound largely healed, he determined that vengeance on the Dragon slayer would be better enjoyed when he had the advantage of rest and clarity.

He could also not deny that Penelope's compelling charm deeply colored his thinking. Try as he might, the mating bond was keenly felt deep within his inner recesses. He resolved to exert his mind against the pull that existed between them, but first, he knew he had to acknowledge it existed.

Much like a wound, the bond they shared would need to be excised, cut away, and cauterized. There was no world in which they were fated to be as one. Experience had taught him that a wound must be tended to, lest infection takes hold.

Evair counseled himself to attend to his immediate needs and address those more pressing matters later. Since Penelope's company was pleasant enough, he did not find the walk through the village as odious as he would have predicted.

Aside from hunger, he knew he needed provisions, clothing and many more trappings of being human. But, as they entered the village proper, he was once again reminded that those 'trappings' had changed much since he last walked above the earth.

Though the village was small, he was dazzled and bemused by the continued abundance of horseless carriages that traveled at an alarming speed. After that first encounter, Penelope did not seem perturbed by their ferocity and speed, so he kept his questions hidden. He did not want to admit he could not fathom just how they moved about with no horse to pull them.

"Are you alright?" Penelope inquired, seeing his face light up in alarm, seemingly at every turn. They were on the fringes of the village, but it was a busy day, and the streets were heavy with mid-day comings and goings.

"I am managing. There have been a few changes since I last encountered a human encampment."

"Yes? How so?"

Evair did not want to recite every maddening, befuddling discovery, so he selected carefully.

"Why are the women so immodestly attired?" His eyes alighted on several women walking through the village, their arms, shoulders and, yes, legs, bared to the sun.

If Penelope was amused by his observation, she concealed it admirably.

"Times have changed since you were here last. Including how modern women dress. Indeed, many things about women have changed."

Evair grunted in response and continued walking, his mind thrumming with tasks he must address. Every time he felt able to convey his ideas, he found himself dodging another meandering human. His sense of self-survival was alarmed at the idea of humans allowing themselves to be so vulnerable to attack. What was in those little devices that kept them from keeping their guard up?

He decided not to ask Penelope, lest she thought his question frivolous.

"I do not intend to infringe upon your hospitality for long. In fact, I should return to Europe to assess my holdings," he stated.

"You have holdings in Europe?" she replied, leading them through the busier main street of Whisper Falls.

"I believe I do. At least, I put such measures into place before my long slumber." Evair chuckled at his foresight. Before he descended into sleep, he had established himself as the heir to his fortune, a roguish piece of knavery designed to take care of his future self. It had the added deliciousness of ensuring heartbreak to would-be pillagers of his wealth.

"I believe I do. I should fly there tonight," he mused aloud, wondering if he could leave Whisper Falls under cover of darkness and whether his wound would impede long-term flight.

"You know," Penelope broke into his thoughts,

"You might not need to fly all the way there to see how things are faring."

"To send a messenger would take too long. I don't intend to burden you to such an extent."

"We don't really do the messengers thing anymore. At least not in the way you're thinking. If you let me help, I believe we could check your holdings here, using the internet. And if that fails, perhaps we can check at the local bank."

Up to this point, Evair believed Penelope was capable of many things. What he did not believe was that some minuscule town outside of Europe would be capable of relaying any pertinent financial information. And what, precisely, *was* the internet? Evair immediately distrusted anything that sounded like a weapon to him.

He was willing to admit that waking up in this new world posed many challenges, but he was certain his wealth was secure. He had ensured that the Drakeson family placed the holdings in banks that would transfer and grow the holdings despite the petty doings of human beings.

Should that fail, he mused (his concentration momentarily flummoxed at the sight of yet another bare-shouldered woman) the hoardings in his underground lair would be ample enough.

A small, squat building came into view, its red brick solid and untouched by Evair's recent tornado.

"Here, why don't we stop in real quickly? We're here after all," Penelope suggested. "Then, at least, you will feel you aren't... infringing on me."

"Yes, let's," Evair agreed, and they stepped out of the sunlight and into the dusty mausoleum-like feel of the bank.

Like most small town banks, it aspired to be more intimidating than it really was, basically a large room with some office space, security boxes, and one large safe. There were only a few tellers at work, with a single banker reviewing loan forms in the side area reserved for client business.

Evair realized it had been many years since he had needed to broker a transaction with a human. Penelope sensed his hesitation and lightly touched his arm.

"Let me help you," she assured, stepping up to the teller's desk.

The teller was a doughy, young man who, like the bank he worked in, believed himself more important than he was. Despite the bank-regulated greeting he issued, his demeanor immediately reminded Evair of someone who thinks they are better than the clientele they assisted.

Evair's insides began to roil with displeasure at the haughty way he looked down upon Penelope. For her part, she did not seem to notice.

"Hello, we'd like to make an account inquiry, if you wouldn't mind."

"Mmm-hmm. What kind?" The teller drew out the words as if Penelope had difficulty understanding him.

"Well, it seems my companion here may have some European holdings, and we'd like to inquire after them. Could you assist us?"

A sigh escaped the teller's lips as if he was being interrupted in his great task of being unpleasant to people. Evair could feel his fists clench, and he had to hold back the desire to shift into his Dragon self and show this insolent human exactly what manners were for.

"Name and address?"

Penelope urged Evair forward to answer the man's questions, stepping away to provide him with privacy.

Evair barked his answers at the teller, clicking his fingernails on the counter in impatience.

After much searching on a large square box

(Evair wondered why he did not consult the large ledger books he was accustomed to seeing), the teller appeared to have located some information. It was apparent in the way he started making a distinct choking sound. It reminded Evair of the last sounds prey makes right before the predator ends their days forever.

"Yes?" Evair inquired, his mood somewhat lightened. "Did you find anything?"

Evair's mood raised even further as he observed the teller's face undergo a great change. Clearly, he had located some pertinent piece of information. Information that was significant, to say the least.

Choking, the teller simply rotated the square into which he had previously been squinting. Finally, a slab of knowledge fell into place for Evair. The squares contained records! Glowing ones at that.

Evair ran his eyes over the effervescent letters and numbers on the surface of the glowing square. Though very distrustful of the box before him, he was satisfied with the numbers. There, he was able to see his name, followed by a number that strung out gloriously far from the decimal point.

Time *had* been kind to the Drakeson family, indeed.

"Thank you. That's all I need to know," Evair turned away from the sputtering teller, who was busy recalibrating his behavior in true sycophant fashion. Evair was used to this routine and looked forward to putting him in his place.

"Perhaps we can get you a bank card?" Penelope broke in. Evair was temporarily annoyed at the interruption of his daydream of torturing the teller but quickly realized her sound thinking. He would need access to his money, and it was clear he needed to know to navigate financially in this new time.

After many attempts to explain the modern banking system, Evair managed to select a pin number (1066). Then, he was ready to leave. The overly attentive ministrations of the teller had grated his nerves beyond his capacity.

"We have completed our business here," he growled at Penelope. "We must leave."

Penelope read his underlying meaning and bid the teller goodbye, who foisted his business card into her hand, urging them both to open something called an IRA. It was all Evair could do not to shift into his Dragon self and tear the building apart.

Once free of the bank, Evair urged Penelope to find food. His hunger was growing, and he was becoming more irritable by the moment. His proximity to these screen-staring, scantily clad humans was wearing thin.

"One more stop before we eat. I promise you, it's worth it," Penelope said, a strange light in her eyes. Despite the pangs in his belly, he was compelled by her smile to follow, stepping into a shop designed to clothe human males.

Once inside, Evair finally encountered something he understood. Being dressed, catered to, and draped like a celestial being was a time-honored tradition in his world. He was more than content to stand still as a tailor, a salesman, and Penelope bustled about him, selecting and discarding an appropriate wardrobe.

Smiling, Evair allowed himself to enjoy the sensation. If he *had* to remain in this human skin suit, he may as well be properly attired. His fortune was finally being put to good use, as only the finest cuts, fabrics and designs would do.

Several minutes later, Evair stood, clad in

cobalt blue dress pants, Italian leather shoes, a lilac dress shirt, and a leather jacket.

Modern tailoring would also take some getting used to, but even Evair had to admit he looked a damn sight more inviting than all the humans he had seen so far.

And yet...

Penelope's visage still pleased and pulled to him. He could not deny it.

He shook his head and admired himself one more time in the mirror.

Hungry, that's all, he told himself.

8
PENELOPE

As she wandered through town with this gorgeous stranger, Penelope was reliving fantasies she thought she had let go a long time ago. When Penelope was still a teenager and brand new to Whisper Falls, she would spend hours dreaming of the day she might turn the corner to see a handsome man walking in her direction, eyes only for her. In the same way she conjured magic between her fingers, she would conjure these stories in her head. Walking hand in hand by the river, showing him small acts of magic to make him smile, and laughing over dinner.

But as the years wore on, Penelope slowly got to know the eligible bachelor pool of Whisper

Falls. And she slowly realized just how unlikely her fairy tale romance would be. Not that she was ever one to wallow. Instead, Penelope had thrown herself into magic, working hard to perfect her skills. She opened her shop and discovered her aptitude for business. And then her dad's health declined. Caring for him had taken up almost all of her energy, and the Apothecary shop had taken up the rest. There hadn't been time for romance in the past few years, and as far as Penelope was concerned, she was all the better for it.

But now, walking next to Evair, feeling the power of him as if it emanated from his skin, she was feeling the whisper of her hopeful, idealistic self. Feelings she had worked hard to suppress were surfacing, and new feelings, like the desire only a grown woman can feel, were also making themselves known. She couldn't help glancing sideways at Evair, wondering if he was feeling this same connection.

Evair shot his gaze in her direction with animal instincts, clearly detecting that he was being watched. All day he had moved with this skittish energy of a defensive animal, like a caged lion or a tiger who suddenly finds himself in the city instead of the jungle.

"What?" Evair asked, looking down at his new clothing, his shoes, maybe even the way he walked. Was that self-consciousness Penelope was seeing? She couldn't help the smile that worked its way to the corners of her mouth.

"Is something wrong?" Evair asked. Suddenly he was moving his feet as if the expensive shoes he wore didn't quite fit. "It's the shoes," he grumbled. "They are all wrong."

"You don't like them?" Penelope asked, but Evair hardly heard. He reached down and pulled off one shoe and then the other, dropping them to the ground and leaving them there as he continued to stride down the street, his long legs carrying him several feet in front of Penelope before she even knew what to do.

"Wait," Penelope called, bending down to gather up the discarded shoes. She couldn't help remembering that the shoes had cost almost as much as her monthly rent on the apothecary shop. She had to run with the shoes cradled in her arms to catch up with Evair, striding along in socked feet.

"There's nothing wrong with the shoes, Evair. I like them! Don't you?" She was still struggling to keep up with Evair, who had picked up his pace, marching along in anger. He was almost... prowling. It was the only word that felt right in Penelope's mind.

"I *don't* like them," Evair grumbled, not looking at her. "I can't feel the earth. And how will I run if someone comes after me?"

His words were full of irritation, confusing Penelope as she struggled to catch up with this strong shift in Evair's mood. He had seemed excited about things earlier. Or had she been the one getting excited? She had certainly enjoyed dressing him up, not to mention spending his money without a care for whether it would run out. Perhaps all this change was just a bit too much for a man who had started his day as a Dragon.

Suddenly, Evair stopped, and Penelope thought he might turn around and apologize, perhaps put his shoes back on. Instead, he reached down and pulled off his socks. With an angry cry that could have been a growl, he hurled the socks away from him, throwing them into the street even as Penelope raced out to retrieve them. She thanked the stars that no one was out in the street to see his childish tantrum.

"Evair," she cried, now holding his shoes and

his socks in her arms. He kept walking, racing ahead of her. In desperation, Penelope mumbled a spell under her breath, and with a flick of her fingers, she sent the magic out to Evair's legs. He stopped, his feet frozen to the ground as she ran up to meet him.

"Evair. It's alright." He was angry, his eyes darting from left to right as he fought against the spell that was holding him in place.

"Let me go," he snarled, but Penelope kept herself firmly planted in front of him, ignoring her fear.

"Look at me," she said gently. Penelope had experience with scared animals and scared little kids. They tended to act just how Evair was acting now: Desperate to flee and lashing out in anger when they were threatened. Miraculously, Evair did as she said, and he looked at her. Their eyes caught one another, and Penelope felt that flutter deep in her stomach, a connection that was pulling her towards this man. His chest was heaving, rhythmically rising up and down, but he was staring at her, and Penelope knew he felt something too. His breath started to slow.

"Good," Penelope said, nodding as she watched

Evair calm down. "Now tell me something. Are you hungry?"

Penelope watched as Evair's brow furrowed, and he scanned his body, paying attention to his stomach. He seemed almost relieved with the realization, as if glad to articulate what was wrong.

"Starving," he answered.

"I thought so."

With a flick of her wrist, Penelope released the bind on Evair's feet.

"Follow me."

PENELOPE TOOK him to *The Founder's Tavern*, thinking the old-world charm and early American décor might comfort Evair a bit. She tried to ignore all the stares they got as they were brought to their table, but part of her relished it. Finally, there was someone else in town who was a bit different. Finally, there was someone else here who was just as interesting as herself. Of course, perhaps they were simply staring at a seven-foot-tall man who wasn't wearing any shoes.

Penelope quickly got Evair seated and slid his shoes under the table. She ordered them both a beer before the hostess could disappear.

"Alright?" She asked, staring across the table at Evair. He was looking around him, taking in the old pictures on the wall that showed scenes of early America. There were politicians Penelope couldn't name shouting out speeches on the floor of Parliament and George Washington on horseback, crossing the Delaware. Evair's eyes caught on the painting just above their table: Benjamin Franklin signing the Declaration of Independence. Suddenly, Evair scoffed and turned away.

"Ben Franklin had a gout flare-up. He didn't sit in the gallery."

Penelope laughed at what she thought was a joke, but the laugh died in her throat as she saw Evair's slight frown at her reaction. He wasn't laughing.

"And how would you know?" Penelope asked, feeling the hint of unease in her chest.

"Because I was there."

Before Penelope could respond, the waitress was back, dropping off their drinks.

"John Adams was whiny. But Franklin was the worst. He slept through half the debates."

Penelope gave the waitress a brief smile, hoping she wasn't listening too closely to the strange things coming out of Evair's mouth. First, a shoeless man walked into the restaurant and now he was spouting off about knowing the founding fathers. As soon as she was out of earshot, Penelope turned her attention back to Evair.

"You were *there?*" She asked, trying to take in the enormity of this information. "At the signing of the Declaration of Independence?"

Evair nodded as he lifted up his beer and gulped down half of it in two sips.

"The signing that happened more than *two hundred* years ago?"

"I was awake for a time, and it was easy to get swept up into that particular moment."

Evair shrugged as if he didn't understand the problem. Clearly, he had no idea about the normal lifespan of a human. And clearly, Penelope was learning a thing or two about the lifespan of a Dragon.

"That's just... I mean..." Penelope was at a loss, trying to wrap her brain around all of those years that Evair had been alive.

"It's... unusual?" Evair asked, finally seeming to grasp Penelope's meaning.

"*Very* unusual. For a human, that is. I know drag..." She stopped herself, knowing it was dangerous to say that word out loud. Not here.

Not where someone from the town might overhear. She took a breath and started again, keeping her voice low and leaning forward.

"I know that *your people* are supposed to live for a long time. But I had no idea it could be... I mean... two hundred years, Evair!"

"More than that," he said coolly. He finished his beer with a final gulp before reaching over to take Penelope's. "I was alive long before Franklin."

With that, he tipped Penelope's beer to his mouth and nearly inhaled it, downing the glass in three giant sips.

"Can we have more of this?" He asked, looking almost confused by the empty glasses in front of him. Penelope couldn't help gaping at him. Not only was this gorgeous man sitting in front of her a *Dragon*. No, as if that wasn't enough, he was maybe three hundred years old. Maybe *more*. For the first time since finding Evair curled up at her feet, she started to wonder what exactly she had gotten herself into.

"Are you alright?" Evair asked. "Are you hungry?"

This made Penelope smile, and the panic that had started to rise in her chest settled down a bit. Sure, he had been around for a long time, but in the world of humans, Evair was little more than a toddler. At least she had a bit of a step up on him there.

"I *am* hungry," Penelope smiled. "Let's see what we want to eat."

9
EVAIR

Within minutes, the table resembled a banquet table from days long gone by. Many glasses, drunk dry with only the cling of a stray foam bubble, littered the space in front of Evair. The waitstaff at *The Founders Tavern* could hardly keep up with him.

Evair enjoyed the cool, frothy brews and did not feel any ill effects from the alcohol. Penelope managed to cordon off one pint for herself and nursed it slowly.

"Do you eat meat?" Penelope inquired, her head obscured by the large paper tablet that seemed to contain the tavern's food offerings.

Evair responded with an arched eyebrow. He was a Dragon of an ancient and noble line of powerful, mysterious creatures. Of course, he ate meat.

Seeing his expression, Penelope blushed a little in embarrassment and went back to perusing the sheet. The beleaguered waitress returned with yet another round of beers. She had begun simply bringing a few at a time to make things more efficient. Evair appreciated this serving human's tenacity.

"Have you decided?" The waitress inquired, blowing a loose lock of hair from her tired face.

"Ah, yes. The steak for him. Rare. With potatoes. And I'll have the shepherd's pie, please."

"Coming right up," the waitress replied, clearing as many empty pint glasses as could fit on her tray.

"Feels strange having a woman order for me," Evair commented, polishing off yet another brew.

"Get used to it. You'll find women do a lot that you haven't seen before," Penelope replied, sipping her beer.

"I only hope your appetite for steak isn't as voracious as it is for beer. I seem to have lost count."

"As have I. I wasn't aware how thirsty I was

until now." He pulled yet again on his beer, draining it.

Now that they were sitting still and some of their immediate needs addressed, an imposing silence descended over their table. Evair had never been one for idle conversation, so he did not attempt it. Penelope seemed content to study him closely, a task he did not actively discourage as he had admitted to himself long ago that he did enjoy when others appraised his physical beauty.

Even as a human, Evair was aware he stood out from the rest. In their short time together in Whisper Falls, he had been made acutely aware that he did not look like the other specimens around him. Inwardly, he smiled at this reflection.

Soon enough, the waitress returned with yet more beer and two plates. Evair was not one to make loud exclamations of pleasure in public, but he could not help licking his lips as the large piece of meat, awash in reddish liquid, was set before him. It was *very* rare indeed, adding to Evair's growing appreciation for Penelope's ordering skills.

The waitress also placed a large steak knife at his place setting. The handle was sturdy, engraved with a simple design that Evair admired at first look.

The blade of the knife had serrated edges but also had a pleasing heft. It tore through the buttery meat easily, and Evair closed his eyes at the twin sensation of the meat in his mouth and the satisfying weight of the knife in his hand.

Penelope had chosen well. If he must dine on human food, *The Founders Tavern* had surpassed his expectations.

They largely ate in silence, broken only by the occasional 'thank you' from Penelope as the waitress continued to replace Evair's beer glasses.

At last, Evair, satiated on almost raw meat, potatoes, asparagus and beer, pushed himself back from the table, a feeling of warmth and contentment on his face. Penelope regarded him intently.

"Am I to believe you have finally filled yourself up?" She asked in a laughing tone, pushing herself back in satisfaction from the heavy deep table.

"For now. I had forgotten that the sensation of eating is a pleasurable one. Thank you for choosing this place." Idly, he picked at a tooth with a long fingernail.

"You are welcome. We don't have many choices

in Whisper Falls, but what food there is, is sure to fill you up. Are you ready to return home?"

"Do you mean *your* home?" His voice lost some of its contented warmth.

He was not eager to pen himself up in her human dwelling in fear. How long he would remain in this human state, he surmised, would have to be a short one. As he had only been awake for a short time now, he wished to get back to how he liked experiencing the world most –as a Dragon people feared and respected.

"I do, yes." Penelope, Evair noticed, kept her tone neutral, causing a twinge of regret to ripple through him. He did not mean to insult her hospitality. In fact, he did not wish to cause her discomfort of any kind.

More pesky thoughts to unearth and cogitate on... when time and space allowed.

Penelope arranged for the bill to arrive, and Evair was quick to exercise his new found banking skills to pay it, signing the paper receipt with relish. As he did so, he thought he detected a sigh of relief haltingly escape Penelope, no doubt due to the rather large charge for the beer he had drunk. No matter, he had the means to pay for a bill like this many times over.

They made their way out of the tavern, Evair glad to connect back to the earth through his feet once more. It was especially potent this time because now he had no gnawing hunger to distract him. He was even able to start to appreciate some of the finer points of the village around him.

As they reached the edge of the large, flat expanse outside the tavern that seemed to be a holding area for the horseless carriages, Penelope laid a hand on Evair's arm.

"Evair. Do you hear that?"

"Hear what?" Instantly, he was on alert, his keen sight scanning the skies overhead and identifying any ambush spots in their immediate vicinity.

"Nothing. It stopped. Sorry," Penelope shook her head, and they continued. Soon, however, she stopped him again.

"There it is again. A clinking sound. Do you hear it?"

Evair zeroed in on the sound, which seemed to stop the second he ceased movement. He reached into his jacket pocket, a small smile crossing his handsome features.

"Oh, you must mean these," he smiled, holding up his fork and the hefty steak knife he had been given in the tavern. At the sight of them, Penelope's eyes widened in alarm.

"What? What are you doing with those? Those don't belong to you!" She scanned her eyes about, trying to keep her voice low. Evair, for the life of him, could not understand her strange behavior.

"Does it matter? They pleased me. I wish to add them to my hoard," he shrugged, recalling fondly the trove that lay beneath the mountain, filled with objects just like these. Metal… precious and not so precious, that had, in some way, pleased him, and thus were added to the collection.

"We just… humans don't do that. You only 'borrow' objects at a restaurant. The food is the only thing they want you to take away."

Evair shrugged again and began walking, but she stopped him with another light touch on his arm.

"You have to go back in there and return them," she admonished, a stern look in her eyes.

"Two things prevent that: my pride and my apathy," he gently shrugged off her arm and started to walk again.

"If you are going to navigate in the human world, you have to play by the rules. You already stand out. Please don't bring any more attention to yourself!"

"It is hardly my fault if humans do not match my... proportions," he leveled with her, already bored of the subject.

"With the amount of money you have, you can buy a truck full of this cheap flatware. I will even help you do it. All I'm asking you is, please return them. We can say it was an honest mistake."

Evair's first instinct was to completely ignore her request, but something deep within him flared in opposition. She had been kind to him, a voice within him reasoned. She had taken him in, healed his wound, fed and aided him. The least he could do would be to comply with her request.

Sighing, he replied to her gaze with the slightest of nods. But he did not wish to have her witness this foolish errand. Similarly, he did not need a woman fighting his battles for him (however small and middling they may be).

Holding up a hand, he urged her to stay where she was as he returned to the tavern and disappeared within its doors. Seeking out the waitress, he discovered her at their table, attempting to balance all the remaining beer glasses into a large tub.

"These. Are... yours," Evair said gruffly, plunking the cutlery on the table. She stared at him for a brief moment, then her eyes flicked to the large collection of glassware, then back again.

Evair detected she was calculating that the beer had hindered his ability to keep flatware to himself.

Turning on his heel, he gave the briefest of smiles.

"Let her think that," he uttered to himself. "Less explaining to do."

Back outside, Penelope smiled, glad to have that awkward episode behind them.

"Change of plan," she said, checking her watch.

"Yes?"

"I have to get to the shop now. I didn't realize the time. I was supposed to open hours ago."

"Are people clamoring for your services?" Evair could barely disguise his disdain for the needs of humans.

"That's the thing. I don't know. But in this town, I'm usually quite busy. And the longer I'm away, the more people talk. That's the last thing we need. Are you alright returning to my house?"

Evair gave her a slow smile. She returned the

look with one of confusion, not able to read his intentions.

"I'm not returning there on my own. I will accompany you. I'm *not* livestock, meant to be stowed away when convenient."

Penelope looked as if she had a retort in mind but quickly seemed to decide against it.

"Fine. Follow me," she said, quickly heading in the opposite direction.

"I intend to," he replied, scratching at his full belly in appreciation.

10
PENELOPE

Penelope made it back to her shop to see a line of people waiting outside of the locked door.

Great. She thought. So much for sneaking Evair into the back before the rest of the town saw him. Instead, it was like the whole line noticed him all at once and turned to see his tall frame and his striking white hair that seemed to shine even brighter in the sun. Penelope ignored the murmurs of the crowd as she pulled Evair along and unlocked the door.

"Thank you for waiting," she called out to the line. "It'll be just a minute."

"Penelope! Who is *this*?" Violet Goldworthy asked as she looked Evair up and down. She was at the front of the line, a wet cloth pressed to her forehead.

"It's alright, Violet. I'll have you inside in just a minute."

Penelope shoved Evair into the shop before closing the door behind them. She had about thirty seconds to give him the lay of the land before the people outside burst in, requiring all of her attention.

"You can wait in the back," she said, taking Evair's forearm to guide him back. But even this briefest of contact caused the couple to freeze in place. Evair looked down at her hand, and the weight of his gaze almost made her shudder. Penelope felt the heat from his arm as if it were fire... both warming her and burning her all at once. Evair looked into her eyes, and the smallest smile appeared at the corner of his mouth.

"Lead the way," he said, his voice low. The invitation felt far too dangerous, and Penelope dropped his arm before fumbling her way forward, casting a hand here and there to turn lights on around her or open cabinets to display her wares. She didn't know why she was showing off like this by using her magic in front of him. She knew it was a frivolous use of something so powerful. But she couldn't help the pride she felt as Evair watched her, a slight expression of awe on his face.

Penelope led Evair to the back room, a small space with a desk where she balanced the books and ordered supplies when the shop was closed. It was small, barely larger than a closet, but it was cozy, and Penelope had outfitted the space with her favorite trinkets and souvenirs from small trips she had taken or items that had belonged to her father.

"You can wait here. I'll take care of this line and then..."

And then what? So far, the order of events had been relatively straightforward. Get the man some clothing and some food, help him navigate the human world, and get his finances in order. But what now? It was clear Evair was financially stable. He could do whatever he wanted and go anywhere he wanted from here on out. Should Penelope say goodbye and send him on his way?

Even thinking that felt wrong. She felt a connection to Evair, and she knew she could never bring herself to wave him off and never see him again.

"And then?" Evair asked. There was another

question there. Something deep and primal that made Penelope blush.

"And then we'll figure out what's next. Just... stay put, alright? A lot of those people look banged up, and I have a feeling you might have been responsible for that."

Evair brushed the thought aside with a roll of his eyes. He took a cool glance around the room before striding over to the chair and sitting down. He stretched his long legs out to rest his feet on the desk.

"Alright," he sighed. "I'll close my eyes for a bit. This new world is a bit too fast-paced for my taste."

And with that, his ice-blue eyes closed, the lids dropping once, twice, and then a third time before settling heavily. His breathing steadied, and he slept, dropping into it faster than Penelope thought possible. Here it was again: the overwhelming evidence that this was more than a human sitting in front of her. He was a creature with the habits of an animal, but the chiseled body that stretched out in front of her was one hundred percent man.

Get a hold of yourself, Penelope thought, shaking her head. She headed back out to the shop, racing to unlock the door and flip the sign to 'Open'. She didn't have time to think about the sleeping Dragon in her office once the townspeople filtered in. She had scrapes and bruises to attend to and Violet's ever-present headache.

"It was that tornado!" Violet cried out, clearly eager for everyone in the store to hear her story. "Those winds were so loud! And the destruction. This headache came back worse than ever, Penny!"

"Alright, Violet. How about something for the nerves?" Penelope asked. She caught a smirk from Mr. Anthony, who stood behind Violet, cradling his left arm.

"The nerves?" Violet cried out as Penelope began looking through drawers to find the small bottle of liquid that had become one of her best sellers. A little something to 'take the edge off' certainly had a wide assortment of uses, and Penelope had learned to keep these small bottles of blue liquid on hand.

"It isn't *nerves*, dear," Violet said. "It's a headache." Violet was looking around the room, suddenly self-conscious that the store was listening to this conversation.

"Of course," Penelope said as she slid the bottle into a paper bag and folded the top. "That's what I meant. This is sure to do the trick for you. A drop or two into your tea whenever you feel..." Penelope stopped herself. "Whenever you feel that headache coming on."

"Well, alright," Violet said, fumbling to find money in her purse. "If you're sure it's the thing for my headaches."

"She is sure," Mr. Anthony chimed in. Violet looked back at him with a glare. She took her change in a huff and stormed out, leaving Penelope and Mr. Anthony to smother their laughter until the woman had pushed her way through the door.

For the next twenty minutes, Violet took care of the line, listening to what was ailing people and prescribing teas or herbs or tinctures that might bring relief. As she suspected, quite a few of her customers had been injured by the tornado Evair had whipped up, and it was the talk throughout the shop.

"What do you think caused it?" Angela Jenkins asked. She didn't seem to be injured as far as Penelope could tell, but Angela was never one to miss out on some gossip. No doubt she was here to listen to the town chatter and gather as much information as she could.

"Too many strange things are going on," Barry

Jenkins answered. He was Angela's husband, and Penelope had noticed that he always seemed to sensationalize any event he could. No wonder Angela was always worked up with the way Barry put ideas into her head.

"First, these rumblings in the earth. Now a tornado. *Something's coming,*" he whispered.

Penelope watched as Angela's eyes grew round and wide, dreaming up all the unspoken 'somethings' that Barry might be referring to.

"Alright, Mr. Jenkins, don't get your wife worked up. What can I help you with?"

As Barry and Angela began explaining what they needed, Penelope caught a tall, white-haired man pass beside her. Evair was awake, and Penelope had hardly gotten through half the line. She kept one eye on him as he slowly made his way around the store, picking up items here and there, smelling something before recoiling and putting it down again. A few people were watching him, their curiosity piqued, but for the most part, he seemed to be blending in. Or blending as much as a tall, exceedingly hot man could in a new town.

Rather than causing a scene by trying to get Evair back to the office, Penelope decided to leave things alone. Perhaps he could keep himself occupied looking at things in the shop until she was able to clear everyone else out.

"It's twenty-five," Penelope said, ringing up Mr. and Mrs. Jenkins. They thanked her and headed out, talking the whole time about the end of the world and evil monsters. Penelope looked up to her next customer with a smile, telling herself to focus. Just a few more people, and she could close up for the day. Then she would figure out what to do with Evair. Suddenly, she felt Evair's looming presence next to her before his hand wrapped tightly around her upper arm.

"What the hell?" She asked as Evair started dragging her out from behind the counter. Penelope was no match for the man's strength, and she was helpless to stop him as he walked her through the store and towards the front door. She felt her face flush red with embarrassment as her customers watched Evair drag her out like some disobedient child.

Evair shoved her through the door before releasing her arm with a shove.

"What's going on?" Penelope asked, reading rage in Evair's expression that had his eyes ablaze. Something had made him angry. Angry enough that Penelope worried he might change then and there back into a Dragon.

Evair threw something at Penelope's feet without a word, kicking up dirt as he did so.

"What is this?"

Penelope looked down to see a simple necklace, one of the novelty items in the shop. They were nothing more than carved designs on a leather string. Flowers or animals that people liked to purchase for gifts since they were made by a local artisan.

"It's just a necklace, Evair. It's worthless."

"This is made of Dragon bone," Evair said, his hands in fists by his sides.

"What?" Penelope asked. Dragon bone was rare, not to mention dangerous. She had read about spells that called for it, but she had always brushed them aside. Until she met Evair, she had been skeptical that Dragons even existed. She never thought she would have Dragon bone in her shop.

"This is Dragon bone!" Evair said again, even more forcefully, so Penelope couldn't miss his words. "How many of my brethren have you slain?"

11
EVAIR

Evair glared at the witch, trying to keep his rage in line. Her cool green eyes looked down on the hideous 'trinket' at her feet and then back up to his face. She was clearly worried, perplexed. It was difficult for him to stay angry while she projected such an aura of distress.

"Evair, I don't know what you're talking about."

She bent down as if to pick up the necklace but withdrew her hand before touching it. He could tell she was torn between picking it up to return it to the shop and leaving it in the dust.

The dirt is where it should stay. It should be buried as befits the Dragon to whom it belonged.

Evair thought of one of his proud brethren, stripped of flesh, scales and wings. Reduced to tiny bones that were carved into ridiculous symbols and then worn around the necks of fools as a decoration. Evair stepped back, feeling horror sweep through his blood and bile rising in his throat.

"Evair?" Penny asked, watching him with concern. She finally bent down and picked up the bone, holding it gently in her hand.

"I cannot... I cannot touch it," Evair said, taking another step back. Nearby, one of those infernal carriages passed by, blowing a cloud of acrid black smoke. The smell turned his stomach still further, and when a noisy flying machine cruised by overhead, he felt a keen urge to bury himself again.

Even if I could step away from Penelope to return to the earth, this injustice would not let me.

Hunters had been stalking Dragons since the beginning of time, and even though it angered Evair, it did not surprise him.

This... This abomination of using our corpses for decoration... This could not be allowed to continue.

"It is, most certainly a Dragon bone, witch," Evair hissed. "You have many on your shelf in there. If you can swear that you did not kill the proud creature to which it belonged, then you must tell me how you came by it."

Penny looked away from him toward the crowd of faces watching them from inside her shop. She gulped, and Evair sensed anxiety in her pheromones.

Maybe, she found it, he thought. This might be ignorance. For the most part, ignorance is inexcusable, but finding a pretty stone and carving it is not the same as willfully robbing a grave or slaying a Dragon.

"I buy materials from a local man named Nestor," she said softly. "He carves these. I thought it was some kind of stone, perhaps the bones of foxes or raccoons."

"Raccoons?" he tried to yell, but his throat was too tight with indignation. It was a good thing, for Evair may have blown away poor Penny, and her shop had his fury come raging out.

"You must take me to this Nestor," he demanded. "Is he a hunter, a slayer of my kind, or a hapless moron scrounging in the woods for treasures he does not understand?"

"Not everything is a plot against your kind," she said gently. "I will take you there if you promise not to eat him immediately. We must give him a chance to explain."

Evair didn't like the way she was talking to him. Her voice had a low, resonant quality, and to his chagrin, it soothed him. He felt calmer, more inclined to listen to her. Evair believed her completely when she said she didn't know and didn't rightly know why. He didn't usually give humans that much leniency.

"We will go now," Evair said firmly.

"No, we will not," she replied gently. "I'm going to go in and serve these customers and close up the shop. It will only take an hour, if not less."

"My people's bodies are hung in your shop like carcasses in a butcher's window, and you want to serve customers instead of going after the monster who is responsible for it?" He asked in disbelief.

She shook her head. "Evair, I must give them some explanation. This is my livelihood. Though it may mean little to you, it is all I've worked for my entire life. Why don't you take down all the bones and anything else you don't like while I send away these people?"

He narrowed his eyes at her, but before he could speak, she turned and walked into the shop, taking the bone with her. She spoke with the people milling about in the shop, apologizing and seeing to their needs. When one old man came forward bent out of shape through the shoulder and neck, Evair saw how much pain he was in and was momentarily distracted.

He tried not to care, but then Penny touched him. Her eyes darkened with genuine hurt. Her hands glowed very subtly, and he knew she was lending some of her precious energy to help him.

I did that.

Evair wandered off into the shop, collecting the necklaces and taking them out the back. He put them all in a sturdy box, thinking that he would like to bury them, but not now. When he had time, he could create a fitting resting place for them. The most important thing right now was to find Nestor and question him fully.

Evair strode back into the shop to see if Penny was working quickly. The need to act was like lightning in his blood. He felt like he couldn't sit still, hands shaking as if his wings were ready to burst forth and carry him straight to the murderer who had defiled his kind. Even as he struggled with his impatience, he found himself admiring her compassion for those she helped.

She spoke to each person with complete focus,

listening carefully to their ills and choosing remedies for them that best suited their injury. Only once or twice did he see her call up her power, and she hid the glow in her hands when she did it.

He realized that she genuinely cared for these people. She wasn't just hanging around here to protect her livelihood, although that was part of it. She wanted to make sure they were cared for before she went to Nestor's.

Evair tried to appreciate how much he had changed her life, but it was beyond him. All he could think about was his duty to his kind, the complete horror of his brethren not just being killed, but their corpses made into trophies. Evair snorted heavily as Penny got to the last customer, sending a small blast of wind through the shop.

Bottles shivered on the shelves, and hanging trinkets danced. The tall woman who was the last customer looked up in alarm.

"Don't worry, Betty," Penny said reassuringly. "I must have left the back window open."

Betty didn't look convinced, but she simply took her bag and left. Penny followed her to the door and quickly locked it. The sun was nearing the horizon now, and even though it was still some time before night darkened the sky, Evair felt that he was running out of time... as if Nestor could evade him in the night.

"Let us go now," he said, his voice ringing around the room. She nodded, sighing. He saw the dark circles under her eyes and the droop of her shoulders, realizing that mortals did not have the same stamina as Dragons.

"You may refresh yourself," he snapped, struggling with the words. "For a few minutes only."

She laughed. "You're such a considerate fellow, Evair," she said. Her comment made him feel quite generous and kind.

"Thank you," he said, puffing out his chest a little. She laughed, and Evair realized there was a joke here that he hadn't gotten. He frowned, ready to ask her to explain, but she stood up quickly and hurried past him to the back of the shop.

She pulled out a small paper sack of cookies and an even smaller box that she drank from. Evair cocked his head at the curious device. It was made of something soft like paper, and the tiny plastic straw stuck out the top like a crooked tree.

"What is that?" he asked, curious in spite of himself.

"It's a breakfast drink. Milky and filling, very

good for when you don't have time to eat a proper meal."

He sniffed suspiciously.

"Smells like a curdled cow," he said in disgust.

She shrugged, eating a cookie. "That sounds about right."

She quickly ate her meal and sucked down the milk, making the little carton gurgle in a way that made him step back in case it exploded. She smiled and shook her head, again withholding modern world knowledge from him. Evair watched her crush the thing in one hand and drop it into the rubbish bin. He looked down on it with a modicum of disdain.

Humans drinking out of tiny boxes, he thought. This modern world was strange to the point of pain, and it was not getting easier for him to absorb. In fact, it was getting downright confounding the more he learned about it.

Penny came out from the small office room, wearing a thick, green jacket. It set off her red hair perfectly, like a forest fire glowing against distant, lush green hills. Evair was struck by her beauty for a few moments.

"Let's go," she said, leading him out the back.

"Remember, you promised not to eat Nestor until we question him."

"I promised no such thing," he said, not trying to hide a haughty tone. If this 'Nestor' looked even slightly guilty, Evair was going to exact whatever punishment seemed fittest. Even that might not be enough to satisfy the slaughter of his kind.

12
PENELOPE

Evair was standing outside the back of the shop, his fingers moving lightly, trickling through the wind. He scowled at the nearby mountains as if his gaze could penetrate the deepening shadows, looking for Dragon hunters and bone thieves, most likely.

"Come on," she said, heading for the car. "Let's go."

He approached slowly, up on the balls of his bare feet, like a stalking cat. Penny stifled a laugh that may have been an expression of annoyance. It was hard to tell at this stage. She'd been on such an emotional rollercoaster it was all starting to feel a bit too much like shock.

Evair danced up to the edge of the car and

touched the door gingerly as if the car might turn and bite him. She sighed again.

"Evair, you have been in the car before."

He shot Penny an anxious look. "Who knows? It may have changed its mind about me by now."

"It's not alive, Evair."

He scoffed at this. "It breathes. I can hear it when you use your magic key to bring it to life. What state does it live in now? Does it feel nothing, or is it sleeping?"

A rush of responses flowed through her, but all of it required a ton of words which she knew would have little effect on his understanding.

"Yes, Evair. It's sleeping."

He nodded, stroking the door. "Wake it up then. I would like to know how it feels before I get in."

She stifled another sigh, opening the door and getting in. The car roared to life as she turned the key, and Evair bravely stood his ground, even though he did jump a bit.

"Easy," he said, stroking the door as he opened it. "Good, metal beast."

"Evair, it can't hurt you!" Penny said, exasperated. He raised his eyebrows as he looked at her.

"I have heard people get killed by these things

all the time."

"Not because they wake up and willfully kill people!" she had to laugh. In fact, she roared with it. When Penny finally stopped, her stomach was sore, and she had to wipe tears from her eyes. Evair was sitting next to her with an almost sullen look on his face.

"I will accept your amusement at my expense," he snapped. "Only if you swear your metal beast will not awaken and turn on me."

"You have my word, Evair," she said, trying to sound solemn. "My metal beast is... ah... Perfectly tame. Well trained."

"I see," he said, stroking the dash. When Penny released the brake and headed out onto the road, he jumped again but didn't look worried, at least.

"How long is the drive?" he asked.

"About an hour," she said, watching the traffic as she headed for the mountain road. Evair snorted, sounding much more like a Dragon than a man.

"Too long to be caught in the jaws of this beast," he muttered.

"Why don't you fly then?" she asked, casually, not looking at him. When she did finally look, he was glaring at her. Penny realized that she may have insulted him, and as they finally turned on the mountain road, she sighed and turned to meet his cool blue eyes.

"I'm sorry. I'm trying to do my best here. You are what humans would call 'high maintenance'."

"I do not understand."

"Praise Jesus for small favors," she whispered.

"Jesus?" Evair said suddenly. "Has that charlatan come again as his followers promised?" Penny was so shocked that she almost drove right off the road on a sharp bend.

"What? You knew Jesus?"

"Of course not," he scoffed. "My race was far too old and proud to mix with his sort. It certainly kicked up quite a fuss with the humans, though. Are they still fighting over the damn book?"

"The Bible?" she asked, incredulous.

"That's the one."

"Well... Yes," she said, thinking it through. "They have even rewritten it several times, so they have more to fight over."

He let out a sharp, sudden laugh. "No wonder he does not want to come back!"

Penny kept her eyes on the road, focusing on following it as the shadows grew. For most of the drive, they didn't talk much, mostly because she was still trying to wrap her head around the fact that her passenger was older than Jesus.

It was near to full dark when they finally pulled up in the clearing near Nestor's cabin. As they got out, a chill wind whistled down from the peaks, stirring Penny's hair. She pointed through the trees, and they could both see the faint light of the dwelling nestled in the trees.

They hurried through the forest, spying Nestor's cabin ahead. There was only one light on out in his shed, and they went straight to it, not bothering to knock on the door. She had a plan of how to ask... gently... how Nestor got the bones, but before Penny could even start, Evair strode in, cutting in front of her and stopping with a regal flourish.

"Explain yourself, Dragon slayer!" he announced. Poor Nestor looked up in alarm. He was sitting at his worktable, his glasses set on his nose as he worked on a delicate sculpture. He handled the bone with the utmost care, his whittling tool honed to a very keen edge. She cursed the fact that he had to be at work at this particular time.

"What?" Nestor asked in alarm. "Who are you?"

Evair strode to the table, his royal bearing

emphasized by the freshly tailored suit he'd purchased. Even his lack of shoes couldn't distract from the magnificent figure he cut.

"You, slayer of my kin, prepare to die."

"Whoa, whoa, wait!" Penny yelled, hurrying up to Evair and putting herself between him and Nestor.

"Nestor, this is Evair."

"Nice to meet you," Nestor answered, a bit sarcastically. His eyes were wide, and Penny could tell he was scared. The poor old guy just pottered about by himself, troubling no one. She couldn't imagine he did any of this on purpose.

"It's always nice to see you, Penny," Nestor said. "But you usually don't bring… Company."

Penny had to admire the easy calm he was displaying. She looked up at Evair and saw his pale eyes blazing with fury as he glared at the old man.

"I'm sorry, Nestor," Penny said gently. "But Evair is a stranger here… He came from far away." She struggled to complete the introduction.

How was I supposed to cover Evair's attitude about the bones?

"Penelope," Evair snapped impatiently. "I should attack right now and interrogate this pathetic creature. Get out of my way."

Nestor's eyebrows went straight up, and he looked between Penny and Evair. He carefully put down his bone knife and the sculpture he was working on. It was far too large to be a necklace, about the length of Penny's forearm. It looked like it would be a mermaid dancing in a wave when it was done, a thing of beauty like all of Nestor's work. She swallowed her discomfort, hoping this really was all just a misunderstanding.

Evair would know Dragon bones... That must be what they are. No matter how beautiful his sculptures are, I can't use them anymore. I might be able to save Nestor's life, though.

She looked up at Evair, and even though his eyes were sparkling with fury, she couldn't believe he would actually eat anyone.

Would he?

Better to never find out.

"Evair. Please, calm down. Take a step back."

He glowered at her, looking down at her hands planted firmly on his chest. He sighed, shaking his head and took one very small step back.

Penny turned to Nestor, who was standing up and had moved away from the table. He was watching Evair like a wild cat might watch a big dog... ready to run at the slightest hint of violence.

"Nestor, I need to know where you get your bones from."

"Bones?" Nestor echoed. "I rarely use them."

She glanced at the table, then back at him.

"Oh! You mean those bones. Of course. I was thinking about something else. Sorry. This is a bit of a shock."

For the briefest of moments, Penny thought she saw a smirk flash across his face. She hid her suspicions, but Evair growled deep in his throat.

"I forage for them in the forest," Nestor said quickly. "Sometimes I don't know what animal they are from. Large ones from bears, perhaps, smaller ones from birds...?"

Evair suddenly sidestepped around Penny, so fast and fluid that she realized standing between him and Nestor was completely inadequate. Evair touched the bone on the counter, and she saw anger flare across his face.

"This bone. Where did you get this bone?" Evair demanded.

"Well, I'm not sure," Nestor said, flustered. "I scavenge all over the peaks and..."

"The peaks?" Evair stepped forward dangerously. "Which peak? Which mountain?"

Penny could feel the situation getting out of

control. She stepped around the desk, trying not to get between them but trying to get close enough to Nestor to hopefully avert disaster.

"Nestor, please. Try to remember. Where did you get this bone?"

His face fell, just a little. He looked at the floor and sighed.

"The ridge that begins about a mile north," he said. "I always find good bones there. I think eagles may die up there, as well as leave their prey after they've eaten. It's always good foraging for an old scavenger like me."

Suddenly, he looked very old and tired, and Penny was sorry to have bothered him. She stepped back towards Evair, who was still glaring at poor Nestor.

"We should go."

"Yes," Evair answered, "We should. But not before we deal with the bone thief."

"Evair, we're done here," she stepped up beside him, grabbing his huge, muscular arm and trying to tug him towards the door.

Evair's nostrils flared. "There is deceit here," he said, turning to glare at her. "Don't you smell it?"

"No," she said, exasperated. "It's probably just fear." Evair nodded, eyeing Nestor again. The old man hung back in the shed, never taking his eyes off Evair.

"It certainly should be," he hissed, growling a little. Nestor jumped, and Penny gasped in frustration.

"I promise you, Evair, if you find any evidence at all, you can return here to decide upon a punishment."

Evair looked at her in disbelief. "Evidence? What more do I need? He has a sacred bone here, in his hands, being defiled by his sharp knife."

Penny's head hurt. She rubbed her eyes, shaking her head. "Let's just check out the ridge," she said tiredly. It would have been one thing to use her magic to determine whether he was telling the truth. Tempting as it was, she'd exhausted herself helping the folks back at the shop. What if she didn't have the strength of reserves to get a proper answer? The old man might fall prey to Evair's anger over nothing.

"Come on," she said. Evair snorted softly but didn't protest. She dragged him towards the door, as much as a petite young woman can drag several hundred pounds of Dragon, wrapped in the skin of a very large man.

13
EVAIR

"I can see the ridge," Evair grumbled as his stomping footsteps carried him over the loam and fallen leaves. "I could fly there before I'd even finished the thought. Yet here am I, *walking.*"

Evair heard a small noise and cast his eyes to his left. Penelope looked innocently back at him. He held the deep suspicion that she'd been laughing at him, but he had not the proof necessary to rebuke her. After all, he might have imagined it, although he didn't think it likely.

"We could return another time," the witch suggested delicately. "As Nestor said, it's a mile away, and the evening will come on sooner than we think."

"No." Evair let loose a low growl to relieve his feelings. "If another of my brethren slumbers there, I must know immediately. Before your local friend does any more violence to my people."

He cast a baleful look over his shoulder to where Nestor's cabin lay in a clearing amongst the trees. It was almost out of sight, but Evair could feel the man's presence.

"Nestor isn't my friend, exactly." Penelope sighed, speeding up her pace so that she drew a few steps ahead of Evair. "I told you, he's a local that I allow to sell his work in my shop. The tourists like it."

"Tourists? What are those? Are they barbarians, that they like jewelry made of bones?" Evair reclaimed the space between himself and Penelope, ensuring in two long strides that he remained at her side. He sent her a glowering look, even though he knew well that she wasn't the source of his frustration.

Something about this situation didn't feel right. Nestor begged innocence, but there had been an undercurrent to his tone that told Evair it was feigned. The man may not have killed the Dragon those bones came from, but he knew more about their provenance than he was saying. Evair reminded himself that he could return to deal with the coward without Penelope's intervention if need be.

"Tourists are people visiting a place for fun," Penelope was explaining. "They like to take home souvenirs. I'm sure that if they knew Nestor's necklaces were whittled from bone, they wouldn't be quite so eager to buy them."

"They wouldn't care. Humans are selfish and weak, without respect for nature or the wondrous ones greater than themselves."

Evair pushed between two trees, annoyed by the feeling of pine needles against his skin. High in the air, he would be caressed by cool breezes, not omnipresent plant matter.

"And I suppose you're included amongst these 'wondrous ones' you speak of?" Penelope didn't wait for Evair's response. "Do you truly think all humans are the same? You seem to have a lot of attitudes towards all humans derived from experiences with only a few."

The witch's brows drew together as she continued to wind her way through the trees. Evair tried not to think about how attractive her face was, even when frowning.

"When those 'experiences' as you call them

nearly resulted in my death, can you chide me for being disdainful of human nobility?" Although Evair refused to back down, he was already regretting his approach. He had no wish to alienate Penelope. In truth, he was having a hard time knowing exactly what he wanted from her. Sometimes, what he wished to do to Penelope was quite the opposite of alienating.

"I healed you," she retorted. "Does your experience with me not count in your tally of human behavior?"

"You are no common human," murmured Evair, lowering his voice. "You are quite... special." He'd intended it as a compliment, but something in him added an unexpectedly sultry edge to his tone.

At the caress in his words, Penelope blushed and angled herself away. The heat in her cheeks echoed in her scent as it warmed and strengthened in the air. Evair breathed in, finding himself even more befuddled as to what he wanted from her. Whether this woman had an inkling of the mating bond or not, she was undeniably attracted to him.

As complicated as it all felt, that attraction swelled within him to a near breaking point. It deepened his own feelings, quenching a bit of the ire he'd harbored over the task at hand. If anything, he found himself looking for the opportunity to make her blush like that again.

No, he told himself. *There are greater things here than simple flirtation.*

The two hiked the rest of the way to the ridge in silence. Evair did not mind Penelope's reticence to reopen the conversation, as the quiet allowed him to stay alert. A few times, the snap of a twig far in the forest captured his attention. Could someone be watching them? Yet, there were no other signs that anything was amiss.

At last, as the blue sky began to be streaked with sunset gold and pink, they reached the ridge Nestor had indicated. In front of them, a meadow spread out towards a cliff face, a drop that left only the open air beyond the carpet of green grass. Evair and Penelope emerged from the tree line, walking to the center of the exposed ridge top.

"Let us investigate," commanded Evair, eyeing the divots and gullies in the ground. "If a Dragon sleeps beneath, yarrow grows upon the soil. Yarrow blooms yellow, but when not flowering, it looks..."

"I know what yarrow is," interrupted Penelope, an amused smile fluttering on her lips. "I run an apothecary, remember?"

"Oh. Yes." For a few seconds, Evair felt almost… flustered. The witch's steady regard of him, her poise and self-confidence, it was all so new to him. He was accustomed to humans viewing him as a threat, or an animal, or a magical myth and their ticket to wealth. He was not used to a beautiful human treating him as an equal.

"How about we start at opposite sides of the meadow and meet in the middle?" Penelope seemed ignorant of the effect she was having on her companion. Tossing back her long glorious hair, she strode across the wildflowers and grass to the tree line farthest from them.

Evair tried not to be irritated that she had walked away before he had agreed to her course of action. He needed to focus. Should one of his people sleep beneath his feet, it was of utmost importance that Evair finds him before another Dragon slayer did.

He pushed away the sliver of hope that he might find where one of his brothers rested and began to trace his way around the stones studding the meadow. Evair moved faster than Penelope, knowing that he would smell the telltale yarrow if he was at all near it.

Soon, he made his way to the craggy outcropping of rock at the other end of the meadow from the cliff-like drop. The bluff loomed over the small ridge, and for a fleeting moment, Evair allowed himself to hope that there might be an entryway to a cave hidden in the stone.

His seeking fingers found nothing but damp rock and lichen. There was nothing there. Disheartened, Evair turned and made his way back to the center of the grassy expanse. Penelope made her way towards him from her section of meadow, the look on her face word enough. She hadn't come across anything that hinted at a somnolent Dragon, either.

"This place is empty," stated Evair when Penelope drew close enough to him. "There are none of my kin here, neither living nor bones."

"I'm sorry, Evair." Penelope put her hand on his arm, and he felt the lightning of her touch strike his heart. Even the merest brush of her fingers made his pulse leap. "Maybe Nestor already scavenged all the bones."

"Perhaps." Evair looked around at the lengthening shadows of the trees, the way the darkness of the forest cradled the meadow. "A Dragon may have died here long ago. It is a good spot for an ambush, surrounded by trees and with the rocks offering high ground."

"An ambush?" Penelope raised her eyebrows. "Don't you think you're overthinking this a little bit, Evair?"

She rubbed a little circle on his arm before dropping her hand. Evair thought that the caress was meant to be reassuring, but it stirred his blood instead. This woman... her skin, her green eyes, her cascading red-gilded hair... she brought his heart to thundering like none ever had.

"Do you have a man?" Evair asked abruptly, surprising himself with his forward question. Her scent and that gentle touch were enough to make him want to sweep her into his arms and plunder those sweet lips. He almost did, except that he did not wish to risk her displeasure.

"Um. That's definitely none of your business." Penelope stiffened, taking a tiny step away from him. "Why would you ask such a thing? We were not discussing my private life."

"Discussion is irrelevant," rumbled Evair, taking a step himself to close the distance Penelope had opened. "I can smell your pheromones when you are near to me. Your attraction is evident."

"You're *sniffing* me?" Penelope took a much

larger step away, appalled. "I– I – I'm not attracted to you," she stammered. "You're just surprising. Unusual. I'm nervous around you at times. Perhaps that is what you detect."

Evair eyed the red flush flooding Penelope's cheeks, and he felt the irresistible pull within him. Even struggling against it was no use... not when she looked as she did at that moment. When her eyes found his again, she froze. Almost without thinking, he reached out, brushing his knuckles along the line of her jaw.

"That isn't... this isn't... We need to be heading back," said Penelope, pushing away Evair's hand. "It's getting dark. I'll have to conjure a light to get us through the forest as it is."

Evair took a deep breath. He could smell the rich warmth of her desire for him, and it was intoxicating. She could use her words to deny it as vehemently as she wanted, but her body wouldn't lie. Penelope stared at him, trembling but not moving away.

Bringing the hand she'd batted aside back to her cheek, Evair cupped her face in his hand. When she didn't pull away, he leaned in, about to bring his lips to hers.

Thunk.

Evair jerked back at the sound. Over Penelope's shoulder, he saw an arrow embedded deep in the ground. No sooner had he registered it than more arrows began to rain down at them. They were coming from the top of the rocks and from the tree line on all sides.

He and Penelope were surrounded.

Reaching for his true form, Evair commanded his body to transform in vain. He struggled again, but his human form clung to him. His proximity to Penelope and his latent desire for her stood between him and the swelling magnificence of his true form. That affection that nearly brought their lips together was landing them squarely in danger.

He pulled Penelope into him, protecting her as best he could, and tried to shift again, fruitlessly. Taking a deep breath, he prepared to attempt shifting one last time, but a new smell entered his nostrils and bought him up short.

Dragonsbane. The arrows were coated in Dragonsbane, the one poison his brethren could not withstand.

This was a Dragon slayer ambush.

14
PENELOPE

It took a second for everything to sink into Penelope's consciousness. One moment, Evair had been leaning into her, looking for all the world like he was about to kiss her. The next, arrows were hitting the grass all around them as Evair lunged to shield her with his own body.

The question of why he cared so much about Penelope's wellbeing crossed her mind, but she ignored it. She ignored, too, the icy blast of fear that gusted through her veins. Why were they being attacked? No one knew they were even here except... Nestor.

Anger at the possibility of his betrayal surged in Penelope's heart, but there wasn't time for it.

She had to act, or all would be lost. As the rain of arrows fell faster and thicker, she blocked out all external distractions and began to chant.

As the string of Latin words dropped from her lips, Penelope began to shape a glowing bubble in her hands. It was a matter of seconds, no more. With the last syllable of her spell, she tossed the bubble up into the air, and it burst, reforming ten times larger around them. Arrows stopped falling all around them, pinging off of the luminous barrier instead.

"We're protected for the moment," she said. Although it felt troublingly good to be ensconced in Evair's warm embrace, Penelope began wiggling out of his arms. She wanted to see what was going on, even if their assailants were hidden.

"You have shielded us." Evair released her and turned his gaze up to look at the sheet of light wrapped around them. There was wonder in his voice. "This is great magic, done well. Can it move with us?"

"Yes, it's anchored to me," replied Penelope. Her answer had barely left her mouth when Evair grabbed her hand and began to run. "Evair," she gasped. "What's going on?"

"Dragon slayers." His face was set, a cold fury in

his eyes that Penelope never wanted to see turned on her. "They mean to kill me with these poisoned arrows."

Penelope swore. The moment she thought she caught a smirk on Nestor's face flashing into her mind's eye. Had he betrayed them, or had someone else followed them here? Could the person that gave Evair the wound she'd healed have been watching them this whole time? That wound had been poisoned, too.

She stumbled, nearly falling to the ground. Fluidly, Evair reached down and swept her into his arms, cradling her against him like she weighed nothing at all. Penelope's heart hammered from being crushed against Evair's chest as much as the terror of the ambush. A new volley of arrows peppered the illuminated boundary of Penelope's protection spell. The missiles came from the direction the two were running toward, causing Evair to pull up short and let loose a howl of frustrated anger.

"They're everywhere," he growled. "We're surrounded, and I can't shift."

"Let's go to the cliff," breathed Penelope. "Maybe we can climb down it. I can use magic to help us."

"We can try," assented Evair, turning on his heel and resuming his gallop, this time towards the end of the meadow.

Suddenly, the near-constant cracking sound of the arrows breaking against Penelope's bubble stopped. The rain of arrows had ceased, right as Evair reached the drop-off. He set Penelope down, all the while looking warily over his shoulder.

"They've stopped," whispered Penelope.

"For now." Evair bared his teeth. "They're planning something. Dragon slayers don't just give up, not unless I've ripped one of their limbs off."

"Uh." Penelope didn't quite know what to say to that and decided to go ahead and examine the cliff beneath them. Nearing the edge, she leaned forward the barest bit, looking out and down.

It was a sheer drop. In the greying light of evening, Penelope could just make out that the cliff fell in a long vertical slab of rock to a gorge far below. Penelope could hear the telltale roar of a river echoing up the mountainside to her ears. Not even with magical assistance did they have any hope of climbing down that merciless precipice.

"Oh no." She stumbled back, tears leaping into her eyes. "We can't get down that way. I've trapped us. Running here was a terrible idea, Evair. I'm so so sorry..."

"There was not a better place to go." He reached out, strong fingers encircling Penelope's wrist. With a gentle tug, he pulled her into his side. "We are no more trapped here than we would be anywhere else."

Penelope shook her head furiously, but before she could settle on any response, there was a new sound.

It was a whistle, and Penelope felt an arrow singe the air past her ear.

"What!? Oh no, oh no, oh no," she gabbled, dropping to her knees. "How are they getting through?"

She reached out, seizing the arrow and ripping it up from where it was buried in the dirt, along with a chunk of grass. Lifting it to her face, she saw a sickly yellow thread writhe around the shaft of the arrow, dissipating as she watched.

"They're enchanted." Penelope held the arrow out towards Evair, shaking it furiously. "Those bastards enchanted their arrows to get through my spell!"

Another arrow screamed through the shield, striking a boulder next to them and sending sparks flying. Fueled by her feelings of helplessness, Penelope snapped the arrow and threw the pieces on the ground.

"It's still slowed the archers down," observed Evair. "They can't send a barrage anymore, not when they have to bewitch each one."

"Thank you for trying to make me feel better, but we're still pinned here," said Penelope, pushing away the despair that threatened to crush her. "Maybe… maybe I can rework the spell to ward off their specific enchantment."

A new arrow struck the ground a few feet from her, and Penelope lunged for it. That same yellow light wound around the arrow shaft. She had a few seconds to examine it before it too disappeared.

"I can do this," she muttered, casting about furiously for another fresh missile. "Just give me a moment. I can…"

She was interrupted by a sickening thwack and a loud grunt. Penelope twisted around and saw an arrow lodged in Evair's calf. With a hiss of pain, he reached down and ripped it out, throwing it to her before she could blink. Blood gushed from the wound, appearing black in the dim light of encroaching night.

"Evair!" Instinctively, Penelope reached for him. She didn't know what she meant to do. All she knew was that she couldn't bear to see him wounded. Her chest throbbed with concern and fear and something that felt like an echo of Evair's own hurt.

"I'll be fine for now," growled Evair. "One arrow isn't enough to kill me, not yet."

"I can heal you as soon as I re-do this protection spell," promised Penelope.

"No," said Evair calmly. "As soon as you redo the spell, you will shelter under it here while I run. They will follow me. I am their target, not you. You will have a chance to escape."

Penelope stared at the man with a Dragon inside his skin. She'd known him for barely a day, but the thought of leaving him behind for the Dragon equivalent of poachers was abhorrent to her. If he left her magical protection, he'd be reduced to a bloodied pincushion in minutes.

"I'm not leaving you." Penelope got to her feet and crossed her arms. "Don't ask me to because I am not!"

Evair narrowed his eyes in displeasure. He opened his mouth, Penelope thought to say something nasty. Those words never came, though, because then a lancing pain shot through Penelope's arm.

She cried out, clapping her palm to the stinging on her shoulder. A trickle of blood welled up through her fingers. The arrow had only grazed her, but there was a burning sensation much larger than the wound should have entailed. The fear that the arrow's poison might be too strong for a human constitution struck Penelope, and once more, she began to speak in Latin.

"You're hurt." Evair's voice filtered into her mind. She made herself stay with the spell, the necessity of searing the poison out of her own veins too strong. But Evair spoke again, his words cold and hard like stone. "You are bleeding. They made you *bleed.*"

A roar of incoherent rage burst from his throat, and Evair changed. Those muscular arms arched into massive leathery wings, and the very human scream of anger transformed into the guttural, root-shaking howl of a mythical beast.

Evair had finally shifted.

With a new cry, this time of triumph, Evair leapt into the air. He darted towards the outcropping of rock at the other end of the field in his Dragon form. Penelope got hold of herself enough to finish her healing spell, but her eyes never left that pearlescent shape.

Evair roared again, and Penelope felt her hair stir at the nape of her neck. Screams echoed through the night as the wind gusted past Penelope, shaking the trees. She could just make out the shapes of humans flying through the air, thrown from the rocks by Evair's windstorm.

He turned his attention to the forest line, sending a vicious and forceful blast of air through the trunks. There were more shrieks and groans from human throats as a wedge of trees crashed down and into each other.

Not waiting to see the end of his handiwork, Evair whirled and gave the same treatment to the opposite side of the meadow. This time, trees were wrenched up by the roots, wheeling up in the sky and off the ridge. Penelope thought she saw a human clinging to the lower branches of one, but she couldn't be sure.

Rearing up in the air, Evair changed direction once more. He flew straight for Penelope, nearing her too quickly for her eyes to take in. She felt a lurching sensation in her diaphragm and gasped.

She was up in the air. Held remarkably gently against a scaled chest, Penelope felt dizzy as the ground fell away from her feet. The powerful beats of Evair's wings reverberated through him and into her bones.

Trembling, she closed her eyes, trying to subdue her vertigo. When she opened them again, Evair was in the midst of setting her down, as carefully as if she was made of glass.

Penelope blinked, realizing from the last yellowed glow of the sun on the horizon that they had flown even farther up the mountain. Much farther, if the chill in the air was any indication. Which meant... they'd gotten away!

Penelope's knees buckled, and she sat down abruptly, head spinning with adrenaline and relief. They'd made it, by some miracle.

Somehow... they were safe.

15
EVAIR

The glory of his Dragon shape flooded him with strength and confidence as he landed neatly next to Penny. The mystery of the change was still strange to Evair, as he wasn't used to flowing back and forth between the two. He looked down on Penny with concern, wishing that he could change at will to hold her in his arms.

"Are you alright?" Evair asked, controlling his breath so he didn't create a gale-force wind that would blow her right off the peak.

"Yes," she said, looking at her shoulder. "It's not deep. It just hurts."

She was far too pale, and Evair knew that she needed warmth, food, and rest. He couldn't provide any of those things up here. They needed a safe place to regroup.

"You can take me home, can't you?" she asked, obviously thinking the same thing that he was. He shook his head, watching her eyes follow his every move.

"We can't go there. They will be waiting."

"Who?" she asked as if she already knew.

"Nestor," he spat, fury making his voice husky. A nasty breeze flickered around him, and he had to rein in his power again.

"You're sure?" she asked, obviously sad. Evair nodded.

"I could tell by the scent. He's been lying to you, Penelope."

She took a deep, shaky breath. One hand stayed clamped on her wound, and he shuffled closer, wishing again for a man's hands so he could help her. He had been insulted by the human shape before but now found himself longing for it. He was surprising himself.

"What are we going to do?" she asked, sounding lost.

He turned his nose up to the sky, reading the wind. It seemed to sing through every scale, a private conversation between Evair and the element that created him. He couldn't smell or sense anyone around them. She would be safe here for a short while if her wounds didn't take too much of her strength.

"Are you well enough to wait here for a time?" He asked.

She nodded, already tearing the sleeve of her shirt to bind it around her wound.

"I can manage. Where will you go?"

"I'll scout around, and I'll check in on your dwelling. If they are this serious about catching me, then they will be looking for us there."

"But will you be safe?" she asked, looking up at him with wide, fearful eyes. Her concern touched him.

"It's dark now," he said. "I can fly in silence without being seen. I won't linger. I'll only see if there is danger and then return to you."

"But what if you can't control the change?" she asked, her voice soft.

"I'll be fine," he said, a little too harshly.

"But you're wounded," she said, gesturing to his leg. It was still bleeding freely, and Evair felt the burn of the poison in his veins.

"It's nothing,". She shook her head, walking towards him on unsteady feet.

"It's not nothing," she whispered, putting out her hands. He shuddered as her skin touched his scales, feeling her power like ice across the heat of the wound.

"Don't," he demanded. "You don't have the strength!"

He could see her trembling as she called for more power. Evair knew that she was weakened, not just from the wound but from the use of her power. He didn't want her to hurt herself just to heal him, but the light flowed from her hands, reaching into his blood. The wound closed and the poison dissipated from his system within seconds.

"Go," she said, staggering back to sit by a small clump of trees that clung stubbornly to the peak. "Go so you can come back quickly."

He had much to say, but in the end, decided to simply go. This situation was mostly out of his control. Evair hated the feeling of being twisted by events beyond his power, but if he wanted to keep Penny safe, he had to act now. She couldn't stay up here forever.

He turned from the peak and launched into the sky. Evair let the exhilaration of flying flood him, glorying in the beat of his wings and the wind screaming around him. Up here on the peaks, it was very strong and unpredictable, but it swept around Evair with the grace and power of a lover. The wind was no enemy to him, not here or ever. He was able to forget some of his fear and uncertainty as he rode the great gusts down into the valley.

His mind kept slipping back to Penelope, waiting on the crest of the mountain. He couldn't focus on the task ahead, as if part of him was still with her. As he came closer to the town, he shook off the feeling, focusing on the darkness surrounding her house.

Penny is well, he told himself. She may be only a human, but she was one of the strongest and most resourceful humans he'd ever met. He had to trust her. That was going to be difficult for him... to trust in another's strength. He had never done it before.

More than a thousand years of only trusting myself... For the first time, this thought seemed sad to him.

Evair circled low over Penny's house, scenting the air. There were Dragon hunters hidden all around her dwelling. He couldn't see any of them, for they had great skill, but he could smell them. As he turned low over a nearby roof, he heard a faint whisper of them speaking to each other.

"...Have to come back here sometime," a faint voice said. Evair was furious enough to try and murder them all, right there and then, but knew Penny would not approve of him destroying the entire neighborhood. He took off... back into the sky, trying to take out his rage on the thermals instead of the hunters.

He flew over the town, staying high enough that he couldn't be seen from the ground. He did a low circle over the shop, scenting the humans huddled in the nearby streets. Evair could hear their weapons as they moved, sensing their menace. Again, his fury rose, tempting him to smite them all where they stood.

He turned his nose back to the peaks, powering up out of the valley to return to Penelope. It was difficult to control himself, especially now that he had the full power of his Dragon body, but he cared too much for Penny to delay.

Or to destroy her shop, he thought. He barely recognized himself as he caught the strong thrust of the mountain wind and let it bear him to the highest point of the range. From there, he spiraled down slowly, focusing on Penny's position.

To his surprise, she had a small fire going, a little red glow reflecting from the rocks that sheltered the peak from the wind. As Evair touched down, he saw that she had arranged some soft, dry grass around the fire to lie down on.

"You're back!" she cried, hurrying over to him. He felt a warmth in his chest that had nothing to do with the fire, and he knew it was the feeling of the mate bond.

Evair struggled against it, even though seeing her in such a domestic setting made it difficult for him. It was not possible for him to be mated, and wild changes to his physical form weren't going to convince him.

Then she touched him. It was a simple, light touch, her palm gently pressing against his nose. Evair felt a horrible sense of vertigo, and then something rushed through him, something that made him feel incredibly sick and dizzy. When he blinked his eyes open and looked around, he was human again. His naked body was pale against the snowy ground.

"Oh," she said, looking at Evair with disappointment. "I didn't mean to do that."

"No, I suppose you didn't," he stood up, looking himself over. At least he wasn't cold. That had to count for something. Just to test the situation, Evair put all his effort into trying to shift. He closed his eyes, clenched his muscles and thought hard about being a Dragon. When he finally opened his eyes, Penny was giving him a strange, amused look. "Would you like to try the Dr. Banner method and just throw yourself off the peak and hope for the best?" she asked, her smile wide and mischievous.

"What?" he asked, feeling like she had just spoken in a foreign language.

"Never mind," she shook her head. "Come and sit by the fire. I regret that there isn't anything to cook over it."

"I can fix that," he said, knowing that he didn't need Dragon fangs to catch a few rabbits. "Give me a moment."

"Evair?" she asked, reaching out for his hand. "What did you find in town?"

He sighed, looking her in the eye. "They are there, Penny. Men are watching your house and your shop."

Her face fell. It hurt him to see how upset she was. The poor girl had her world destroyed over and over again in the course of a day. Evair could relate. It was only now that it occurred to him that they were very alike in that way.

All we have is each other.

Evair refused to entertain that thought. "Make yourself comfortable," he said, turning to head into the nearby scrub. "I'll be back in a few minutes."

Evair shrugged the tension out of his shoulders, twisting his head into the wind. There was prey nearby, and he was grateful that his instincts and senses were still as keen as his Dragon's. He had promised her food for her fire.

What kind of man would I be if I failed to provide for such a fine woman?

Not a man at all, he thought, the irony not lost on him in the slightest.

16
PENELOPE

She headed back to the fire, feeling somewhat lost. Evair was difficult to read and not an easy talker. Without him being able to shift, they were stuck up here. There was no way she was going to try and hike down in the dark.

Penny wondered if he really could catch rabbits in his human shape. It would be interesting to watch him charging through the thickets naked. She covered her mouth and giggled as she sat down.

It stung bitterly to discover that Nestor had betrayed her. Not just the ambush, but that there were hunters around her house. He had always seemed like such a kindly old fellow. She would bet on him killing her just to get to Evair... or maybe even just killing her for spite.

Penny didn't have much time to contemplate before Evair returned with three rabbits hanging from his fist. She was surprised enough that it took her focus off his nudity.

"How did you do that?" She asked. He grinned.

"Ingenuity! My senses are heightened beyond a human's, I think. These are young rabbits, anyhow. They weren't good at evading a predator." he sat down by her side, looking at the rabbits in consternation.

"I'm not sure how to dress them without my claws."

He sounded stubborn and slightly forlorn at the same time. Penny pulled out a knife that she kept strapped to her calf.

"Here," she said, reaching out to take one. "I can probably use my magic to skin them if the knife isn't sharp enough."

"You will not!" he said firmly. "You will never heal that wound if you keep drawing on your energy. You will wait for me to skin them."

She wanted to protest, but he was so certain, so furious that she relented. Penny realized that he was desperately struggling for control, and she had to let him have it. She couldn't imagine the feeling of having so much power, only to have it ripped away by forces beyond her comprehension. Not so long ago, *Dragons* had been beyond her comprehension. The thing she had to remember was that he was also a man now.

Her eyes sank down towards his lap, and she had to cover her giddy grin. Yes, he was very clearly a man right now. The cold didn't diminish him at all. He didn't even shiver as the wind took on a nasty bite.

Penny watched him clean the rabbits, his deft movements with the knife skinning them quickly and thoroughly. It wasn't a particularly sharp knife, but he had very strong hands. Her eyes lingered on those hands as he found a couple of sticks and spitted the plumpest pieces to hold above the flames.

"I've never done this before," he said, with the air of a man letting go of a great secret. Penny felt a connection inside her, a magnetism that drew her towards him. He was showing vulnerability, and it touched her deeply.

"Don't hold it too close," she said. "It will burn. Just hold it a little higher, then the flesh inside has a chance to cook before the outside burns."

"Who taught you?" he asked. Penny had to swallow a lump in her throat before answering.

"My father," she said softly. Evair's pale eyes turned on her, focusing sharply.

"You have been without him for some time?"

She nodded, not feeling that her voice was strong enough to speak. Her mind was flooded with the images of her ordinary, everyday life, which she now saw as a pointless exercise of keeping busy while she ran from grief.

"You're lonely," he said as if it were a revelation. Penny wanted to protest, but he was right. She had only just realized it, but she had been desperately lonely.

Penny nodded as he pulled the makeshift kebabs from the fire. They ate slowly, savoring the meat. She felt her strength growing at every bite as if she could feel herself healing. She would have her powers back in full very soon. Even then, she wouldn't attempt to get down the mountain until dawn was near.

"What is the cause of your loneliness?" Her eyes flashed up to find him watching her intently. "If it's not too bold a question." There was something uncharacteristically gentle in the way he broached it.

"I came here to care for my father when he was ill. As he got worse, it became the center of my life. By the time I finally lost him, I realized that I hadn't taken the time to know anyone. Some people have come into my life since then, but..."

"Nothing to fill the absence," Evair finished.

"Yeah," she nodded. "Do you get lonely?" His brow furrowed at her question, and she almost regretted asking. It was so hard to tell what was going to send him to darker thoughts.

"Loneliness is part of who we are. How we are. Until we find someone who understands. A kinship that breaks through." His eyes found hers, and a strange frisson in her chest caught her breath. "Until such a kinship comes, one doesn't recognize loneliness. It's just our way of being."

"Do you recognize it now?" It was a daring thing to ask, and his reaction answered for him. He knew. For a moment, they both turned their attention back to their food, but Penelope couldn't shake that prickle behind her sternum.

"I'm not lonely now," she said, feeling bold. He turned to look at her in surprise.

"I do not think that I am good company," he said in a chiding tone. "I've slumbered under a mountain for more years than you've been alive. I wasn't fond of humans before that. Why should I feel like comfort to you?"

"I don't know," she said, covering his hand with hers. "But I feel something."

Her voice broke, and a tear ran down her cheek. This was all so shocking and sudden it could only be a complete disaster... Or true love. Right now, Penny didn't care which. She just wanted him to hold her and make her feel better.

Be my fantasy, even if it is just for tonight.

He looked down at their joined hands, then up into her face. There was no hiding the fact that he was aroused. He noticed Penny looking and grinned, not even shamed enough to blush. She grinned back, feeling light and carefree, like a teenager.

That's just shock...

It very well could be, but she didn't care. This whole thing was crazy. It was time to give herself up to it.

Before she could move, Evair leaned forward and kissed her. He approached carefully, not imposing on her space. She had to lean forward to meet him halfway.

Their lips touched, and there was a flare of magic. It burned her and made her skin tingle. A sudden breeze buffeted them, making the fire spin crazily. They both paused, trying to pull apart, but the magnetism dragged them back together.

Penny leaned into him, letting go of his hand so she could grab his shoulders. She thought he was going to back away when suddenly she felt his hands go around her waist as he pulled her forward. They toppled over and landed with Penny straddling him.

She focused on his lips on hers and nothing else. His body was hard and hot beneath her, and his hands were moving across her body with a sensation that could only be described as magic. She felt more excited than she had ever been, a fierce arousal that started between her legs and crested to flow across her entire body. Penny moaned and writhed in his arms, kissing him with more passion than she'd ever felt in her entire life.

This is what it means to be swept away... she'd given up on it ever happening to her. Impossible, she had always said. A stupid fairy tale. No man could be that good.

But he isn't even a man...

His hands gripped her around the waist, and he flipped them, using his great strength to pin her to the ground. He pawed his way through her jacket and blouse, groping at her breasts. She writhed on the ground, urging him on. When he plunged one hand between her legs and rubbed her there, she shrieked with so much power it rang around the peak, the echo of her pleasure chasing itself across the wind.

He grinned, kissing her hard and grinding his hips against her. Penny put her hands on his cheeks, stroking his face to link her wrists behind his head and kiss him with ferocious desire. Her body bowed under his strength, and for a few moments, she ceased to be anything except delicious sensation.

He paused, looking down on her with an unfathomable look. She wondered what was wrong, why he had stopped. He ran his fingers lightly down her chest, the barest line of skin showing through the open jacket. When his hand reached her pants, he cocked one eyebrow in a wordless question. She nodded breathlessly.

He unbuttoned her pants, grabbing the waistband with both hands to tug them down. He was so strong that she heard threads breaking but didn't care. She was writhing on the ground, trying to help him. He barely got them halfway down her thighs before he bent his head and pressed his lips to her aching clit.

This time the scream that poured out of her clamored around the peak, challenging the howl of the wind. His hands crept around her hips, squeezing her butt as he held her against his mouth. The movement of his lips sparked explosions of pleasure that jolted through her, making her squirm. He held Penny with his boundless strength and kept pressing his tongue further into her pussy.

With a grunt of frustration, he grabbed the waistband of Penny's pants and wrenched it downwards again, bringing them to her knees. She kicked savagely, trying to free herself of at least one leg so she could part her thighs for him. He plunged his head down, moaning as his lips and tongue finally found the deep slit and delved into it as if he were biting into a succulent fruit.

Penny grabbed the back of his head, sinking her fingers into his long, silky hair. Her hips moved of their own accord, thrusting up and down against the pressure of his mouth. She threw her head back, looking up into the endless sky. The tiny, crystal sparks of the stars seemed to dance in joy above her head.

It was as if all was right with the world. Penny couldn't describe it. She could only know it. She was where she was meant to be.

In his arms. From now until forever. No thought existed here, no excuses and no reason. There was only passion, lust, and desire.

17
EVAIR

Evair's senses were filled with her. This woman who lay before him, baring herself in the most intimate way. Welcoming his attentions.

Penelope.

He knew this was a gift and that he must treasure her sharing of her body. It was not a hard task, as her curves were those of a goddess to him. The pale skin of her thighs, the glorious rounding of her hips. Her taste.

Evair had never tasted a nectar as sweet and rich as Penelope's in all his centuries of life. With each lap of his tongue at her core, he reveled in the way her arousal coated his mouth anew. The warmth of her and the way his lips slid over her slick folds gave him endless pleasure.

His ministrations gave Penelope pleasure, too. That was unmistakable. She trembled beneath him, a light mist of sweat rising to that perfect skin. With each lick at her core, her breathy moans built louder and louder.

The sounds of Penelope's desire sent heat arrowing between Evair's legs. He didn't think the stiff member between his legs could grow any harder, but with every gasp and groan from Penelope, he was proven wrong.

"You are perfect," murmured Evair, letting his lips brush ever so lightly against Penelope's core as he spoke. She writhed at the torment, bucking her hips in need Evair grinned at this new proof of his effect on her. Instead of doing as she wished and plunging his mouth back down on her clit, he ran the tip of his tongue up and down her slit.

"Evair!" Penelope cried out, his name a plea in her mouth. "Oh my god, Evair, please!"

"Please what," he growled, kneading her thighs with his thumbs. He allowed the stroke of his fingers to near her sensitive core but never directly touched the swollen button between her legs. He was teasing himself as much as Penelope, so desperate was he to lave her with his tongue once again.

"Please," she begged. "I... I... I need you."

That admission was all it took. Hearing this gorgeous woman who sent magic surging through his veins say she needed him? It was as good as a drug for Evair, sending him into a frenzy of passion.

He pressed his mouth to her clit, sucking and licking as though he'd never stop. As Penelope screamed her pleasure into the night air, Evair slid his hand between her legs. Her slick moisture coated his fingers as he explored her tight opening.

His cock throbbed as he let the tip of his finger slide into her soft warmth. Her body clenched around him as he pushed deeper and deeper into her cavern.

"Yes," gasped Penelope. "Don't stop, please don't stop."

Evair had not the slightest intention of stopping. He sensed that his lover was close to a precipice from the way her body shook beneath him. It was like electricity coursed through her, sparked by his lips and his touch.

He felt powerful but not at all in the way he was accustomed to. It wasn't the violent, brute strength of fighting in his Dragon form. It was like the power of flame, so unique in its ability to both warm and consume.

Penelope shrieked as she reached the pinnacle. Her body twisted beneath him as delirium wracked her every limb. Evair greedily drank up the flood of wetness that soaked her folds, wringing every drop of ecstasy from her that he could.

The orgasm subsided, leaving Penelope panting and supple beneath Evair's hands. Yet, he wasn't finished by any means. His swollen erection was insistent, as was the pulse of his heart. The urge to possess his destined mate and complete the mating bond was overpowering.

"Penelope," he said, his voice rough and low. "May I join my body to yours?"

Her eyes bright, she nodded. That was all Evair needed.

He drove himself into her. With one fluid thrust, he pushed his cock all the way inside. His hips were flush against Penelope's as her walls grabbed his thick length with exquisite tightness.

"You're mine," he murmured, the words falling from his lips unbidden. "You're everything."

A new flare of magic rushed through Evair. It

was akin to the one he'd experienced when they kissed earlier, and yet it was so much more. He felt for a moment like his bones were wreathed in light. The stars come down to reside in his heart.

Overcome, Evair dropped his head and kissed Penelope. He plundered her delectable mouth with his tongue as he began to move inside her. She reared up, wrapping her arms around his neck as they melded their lips together.

Each rock of his hips sent waves of delight crashing through Evair. He'd never experienced anything like this sensation. He never wanted it to stop, never wanted to be any further than this from his Penelope's embrace.

Not for the first time that night, Evair felt an abiding gratitude for his human shape. He'd considered it so weak and vulnerable, but he was learning that it carried a different kind of strength. His human body was matched to Penelope. Not only could he hold her in human form, but he could also join himself with her and take them both to a realm of shared joy.

They moved as one, Evair finding a rhythm that took over his every muscle. With each draw back, he felt the loss of Penelope's snug velvet around his shaft. With every plunge forward, he shuddered with satisfaction.

He broke their kiss, dragging his lips from Penelope's mouth and down to worship the line of her neck. He trailed under her jaw then down her throat. Her pulse thundered against his mouth, beating as fast as his. Evair let himself fall into the sound of her heart for a moment before moving to her shoulders.

Finding her collarbone, his blunt teeth gently nipped at it. Penelope let out a moan, her channel convulsing around his member. Evair groaned back and began to drive himself into her harder and faster. Everything was building within him, almost too much for his skin to hold.

Yet, he wanted Penelope to feel the same way. He wanted to draw another orgasm from her glorious frame, hear her call his name.

Putting all of his weight on one arm, he kept himself propped above her while gliding his hand down to where they were joined. The pad of his thumb found her most sensitive spot, pressing into the swollen cluster of nerves.

She gasped and bucked into his hand, wild with enthusiasm for his touch. Holding back the tsunami that threatened to engulf him, Evair began to rub slow, hard circles against Penelope's clit. He could feel her reacting as her walls quaked around his length.

Their lovemaking reached a fever pitch. It was as though the air around them thrummed, filled with the magic of desire. They were connected at many points, their bodies knowing what to do better than their hearts.

With one final caress, Penelope cried out beneath Evair. Tremors ran through her as her passion crested, and she sobbed his name to the winds. Hearing her call for him at the zenith of her ecstasy was the sweetest sound Evair had ever heard.

He buried himself in her, roaring as he exploded. His cock pulsed as he released his hot seed deep within her, emptying himself completely. A scorching and wonderful rush ran over him, leaving banked flames in its wake.

Evair slumped over Penelope, catching himself before he could fall on her. Sliding to her side, he laid down on the grasses she'd arranged. She must have charmed them because they felt soft and warm.

Reaching for Penelope's waist, he drew her into him. She fit into his side perfectly, her curves molding to his angles. Her head came down to rest on the muscles of his chest, and she gave a quiet little sigh of contentment.

In the way that her sounds of pleasure drew pleasure from Evair, her sound of happiness made the same emotion surge through his heart. He felt a tenderness he'd never known before and found himself pressing a kiss to the top of her head.

Then, he caught himself. He was behaving like a lovelorn swain after no more than a day with this woman. While he had only to reach to sense the mating bond shimmering between them, he could not let himself acknowledge its presence.

Certainly, the sharing of their bodies had been incredible. The way Penelope made Evair feel... it defied the limits of belief. However, he refused to wholeheartedly embrace the idea that the witch was his fated mate.

It was unheard of amongst the Dragons. Fated mates were rare, but human mates? Impossible. Whatever magic compelled Evair towards Penelope, he could not accept that it was that of a mating bond.

As his mind roiled with confusion and haughty resistance, Penelope shivered. Evair was not so trapped in his own conflict that he did not register this, and he lifted his head in mild concern.

"Are you cold?"

"A little," admitted Penelope. "You're quite the furnace, but, um… I am naked from the waist down, and it *is* a little breezy up here. Are you somehow not cold?"

"I do not feel the temperature," explained Evair, trying to keep his tone warm but not overly intimate. He had no wish to hurt Penelope by behaving boorishly after what just happened between them, but neither did he want to seem the eager lover.

"Lucky you." Penelope rolled up to sit, clearly looking around for the pants he'd so unceremoniously removed from her legs. They lay a few feet away, illuminated by the firelight. Penelope reached for them but stopped, frowning.

"Evair," she asked slowly. "What is this?"

She turned to him, and in the light of the flickering flames, he saw the stylized shape of a Dragon low on her abdomen. She rubbed her finger over the lines of the shape, but they remained unbroken, strong and deep blue.

"This better not be some kind of Dragon STD," she said, alarm in her voice.

"No, no," he reassured her, eyeing the tattoo distrustfully. He knew what it meant and yet told himself it had no business marking Penelope. "It won't hurt you. It is simply the mark of laying with a Dragon. It will likely fade."

Part of him knew he was lying, while another part of him was certain that he spoke the plain truth. He took a deep breath, meeting her eyes.

"It's nothing, Penelope."

18
PENELOPE

Penelope woke wrapped in Evair's arms. The sunlight streamed down on her face, and she yawned, snuggling closer into his warm chest.

For some reason, it didn't strike her as odd that she felt so comfortable in Evair's embrace. However, she was troubled to realize that she couldn't quite remember how the previous night had ended. She remembered part of it *very* well, to the extent that her face heated as she recalled the sight of Evair's head between her legs.

A crisp morning breeze snaked around Penelope's shoulders, sneaking under her jacket and making her shiver. The chill reminded her that she'd been cold last night, despite Evair's warmth. She'd put on her pants and then…

That was it. Penelope had used the rest of her strength to cast an insulating spell around their fire. She'd laced the casting with protective enchantments that would warn them of any human's approach so that both she and Evair could get some sleep.

Her working had used up the slim remnant of her strength. Penelope dimly recollected her vision going blurry at the corners and a slow crumple to the ground. She thought Evair had caught her at the last moment but only remembered a pleasant sense of safety.

"Penelope, you are awake." Evair's deep voice rumbled through his chest, comforting against Penelope's cheek. "I can tell by your breathing."

The witch didn't quite know what to say to that, so she pulled away and sat up.

"Yes, I'm awake," she said, even though Evair's words hadn't been a question. "Did you sleep at all?"

"Some." Evair shrugged and got fluidly to his feet. "Once your spell dissipated, I felt it important to stay alert and keep watch."

"Oh. Thank you for, um... doing that." Penelope tried to avert her gaze without being too obvious about it. Evair stood in front of her, magnificent in his nudity. Now that she'd had her hands on him, his naked body was even more distracting.

"We should return to my house," suggested Penelope, carefully not looking down. "We can't stay up here forever. We have no supplies, and you have no clothes."

"I still cannot shift," retorted Evair, seemingly at odds with himself. "I tried once in the night, but..." He looked at her, and there was an air of vulnerable admission in his next words, "I cannot fly us back to the town."

"Then we'll just have to hike down," replied Penelope reasonably. "I've foraged for herbs in these mountains many times, and I know we can manage."

Evair glowered, crossing his arms in displeasure. It suddenly occurred to Penelope that he was going to be hiking down the mountain naked. Trying to smother the blush that rose in her cheeks at the thought of following his sculpted backside down the trail, she turned on her heel and began to walk.

Their journey down the mountain took nearly four hours. Lucky for Penelope's sense of decency, they didn't run into anyone else, even when she found a more maintained trail. Evair seemed pensive, giving only vague, brief answers when she attempted to start a conversation.

Penelope didn't mind. She could barely keep her composure together, weaving through the trees next to seven feet of gorgeous male. There was no safe place to look. Even training her eyes at his shoulders sent desire humming through her. She couldn't help but admire the way his corded muscles moved under his smooth skin and think about how it felt to have that physique on top of her.

Thankfully, they made it back to Nestor's cabin without incident. Evair went into high alert the moment the clearing came into view, but after a few deep breaths, he confirmed that Nestor was not anywhere nearby.

Penelope hurried to the car, hoping her standard enchantments on it had held. There were scratches around the doors like someone had tried to pry them open, but otherwise, the car was intact.

"Is your metal beast healthy?" asked Evair,

coming to stand next to her after a wary circle around the cabin.

"I believe so," Penelope spoke three words of Latin and tossed a light charm over the car. It returned no evidence of sabotage, so she got out her keys and unlocked it. "Yes, the car is just fine."

"Does it resent being left in the lands of the enemy?" Evair cocked his head and stroked the hood of the car before getting in.

"Cars don't really have feelings," Penelope explained as she gunned the engine. The sooner they were away from Nestor's cabin, the better. "I promise, it may seem alive, but it's a machine."

"I know what machines are." Evair gave a low 'humph' and turned to stare at the trees whizzing past the window. "Printing presses and such things. They do not move of their own accord."

"Well, I'm driving the car, though," persisted Penelope.

"Exactly. It is akin to guiding a horse, not operating machinery."

Penelope decided to give up on making Evair understand cars once again. She wondered how he could be that stubborn when it came to change after living through so much history.

Once they reached the outskirts of Whisper

Falls, Penelope pulled into the tiny parking lot of a vacant storefront.

"How do you plan to evade the Dragon slayers?" asked Evair abruptly. "Do you imagine they will have dispersed? I promise you, they will be right where I left them."

"I know." Penelope stretched, her muscles tight after the hike. "I'm going to go confront them. It's the middle of the afternoon. They aren't going to attack me in broad daylight. While I distract them, you can sneak in through the back door. I'll cast a temporary invisibility spell on you."

"I do not like this plan," replied Evair, brows furrowed. "I… do not want you hurt. They are after me, and it is only because of me that you are in this predicament."

"Is that what you've been stewing on all day?" Penelope looked at him with curiosity. "Are you working yourself into being guilty over all this?"

"I am not *guilty*," said Evair, shoulders stiffening. "I am, however, the reason that armed men are surrounding your place of residence."

"Evair," began Penelope, exasperated and strangely a little hurt that he didn't think of them as a team after the events of yesterday. "It's too late to change anything, and even if it weren't, I would still be helping you."

A softness came into Evair's eyes that tugged at the witch. She saw real concern for her in his gaze, beneath the stuffy nonsense about him being to blame for the Dragon slayers.

"Stay here for twenty minutes," she told him, gentling her voice and laying her hand on his. "After that, head to my place, but be careful. Okay?"

"Alright." Evair agreed, but he didn't look happy. "If you are in danger, scream, and I swear, I will come to you."

For a moment, Penelope thought Evair was going to kiss her. Part of her yearned for the touch of his lips, but another part demanded that she stay focused. Yet in the end, that was irrelevant, as Evair leaned back into his seat, face stoic.

It took Penelope only a moment to throw an invisibility spell on him, although it was a use of magic she wished she didn't have to do. Leaving Evair sitting in what to all eyes was an empty car, she hurried towards her house.

She'd be damned if it wasn't Barry Jenkins lounging against a street lamp on her corner. He saw her and straightened, immediately sticking his fingers in his mouth and releasing a long, loud whistle.

"Alerting the rest of the creeps staking out my house?" asked Penelope mildly, continuing to walk towards her door.

"Where's your Dragon boy toy, Cloverlid?" Barry followed her menacingly, and she had to stifle a laugh at how hard he was trying to play the tough guy.

"He's not here anymore," she retorted, putting some steel in her words. "And why are you trying to kill him anyway?"

Two more local men skidded up to them, followed by Nestor. Penelope's stomach turned at the sight of his deceitful face, the smile on it mocking her.

"You're a traitor," hissed Trevor Farthingale, using his bulk to block Penelope's doorway. "How could you side with a Dragon against your own kind? Don't you know they're evil?"

"Funny, if anyone is evil, I think it must be you," snapped the witch. "Harassing an innocent woman and attempting to kill a Dragon who's done nothing to hurt you."

"Done nothing?" Nestor stepped forward, his smirk becoming a snarl. "Dragons are dangerous, you stupid bitch. It must be slain before it devours the entire town."

"I don't really think that's an accurate assessment, Nestor." Penelope whirled around to find an older man she'd never seen before hustling toward them.

"Shut the fuck up, Fetterson," Nestor sneered. "It's your meddling that got Walker's back broken."

"I didn't know he wanted to kill the Dragon," Fetterson fretted. "He told me it was for research."

"And we're all grateful. Now somebody get this fat prick out of here before he gets somebody else hurt." Nestor looked among his flunkies, and one of them ushered the protesting old man away. Penelope almost felt sorry for someone who had so clearly been used, but she had bigger problems.

"Now," Nestor said, turning all of his attention back to Penelope. "You need to start talking, little lady. If you tell us where the Dragon is, who knows? You might even stand to profit from our little hunt."

"You know? If you don't stop harassing me, I might just let Evair eat you!" She muttered a word in Latin and light sprang to her hands. "Or maybe I ought to just hex you myself."

"Listen, you silly little… " began Nestor, but a new voice interrupted him.

"Oh, PENNY!" Violet Goldworthy bustled towards their little group. "I'm so glad you're back! I saw that your shop was still closed this morning and my *word*... I was so frightened something had happened to you! Is everything alright, dear?"

Violet, drawing herself up in surprisingly imposing fashion, made her way right to Penelope, eyeing the men around them with distrust.

"I'm fine, Violet. Thank you for worrying about me," said Penelope, reaching out to squeeze the older woman's hand. "These gentlemen were also very upset by my absence and are demanding I help them this instant."

"Well, goodness gracious!" Violet was speaking loudly now and glaring at the men. "Give the poor girl a break! She isn't at your beck and call, you know!"

"It was urgent," mumbled Barry Jenkins, looking sheepish.

"It can't be that terribly urgent," retorted Violet, looking him up and down. "I see no blood. Now you can just let darling Penny have a day off and consult her tomorrow like the rest of us."

Violet's performance had drawn quite a few

stares, and between her bristling and the interested looks of other passersby, the Dragon slayers shrank a little.

"Thank you, Violet," said Penelope, really meaning it. "Now, if you'll excuse me, gentlemen, I would like to go into my house, please."

"We'll be back," hissed Nestor, the threat barely veiled. His eyes were cold and dead as they locked on the witch.

"Now really," huffed Violet, but the men were already walking away.

Relief flooded Penelope, enough to make her feel a little weak with it.

"Thank you again, Violet." She kissed the older woman's cheek. "Now, I really must be going."

"Of course, of course." Violet flapped her hands, staring after the retreating Dragon slayers with a troubled look. "I don't know what men are coming to these days, so rude!"

With a murmured goodbye, Penelope took her leave of Violet and slipped in the door. She closed it and leaned her back against it, breathing out.

The air in front of her shimmered. In a feat of truly perfect timing, her invisibility spell evaporated, and Evair stood in front of her.

"You *should* let me eat them," he told her, his

expression stormy. "The next time I'm in Dragon form, I could easily crunch their bones."

"No," said Penelope, pushing herself away from the door. "Come on. We need to pack up as fast as we can. It's time to get the hell out of Whisper Falls."

19
EVAIR

"Be at the ready for anything," was all Evair said as he scanned the area surrounding Penelope's dwelling. The only movement was a slight fluttering of tree branches in the gentle wind. Evair knew not to take comfort from such moments of calm. In his experience, they usually boded poorly, and letting one's guard down could be deadly.

Penelope, meanwhile, moved quickly and silently through her house, selecting and discarding items to pack into a sturdy backpack. From his vantage point, Evair made sure to keep one eye on her (he found he could not help himself), and he appreciated how she chose the practical over the frivolous.

It was clear she was a survivor. And a fighter. And a formidable one at that.

It was also clear there would be no rest tonight. Even though the view outside the window appeared calm, he knew that could change. Sleeping would not be advisable, nor could he if he wanted to. He doubted Penelope would be able to rest either. But, while it was quiet, he intended to offer her the chance.

The Dragon slayers seemed like an unstoppable and ever-replenishing source. Although he could blow them off mountains or threaten them, they just seemed to proliferate when his back was turned.

Like vermin...

"Just about packed," Penelope called, her voice steady and sure. He wondered what was running through her head. After all, in the last few days, her entire life had been upended. He was only now coming to realize just how discombobulating that might be for her.

Yet, she betrayed no sense of loss, regret, or blame. He was grateful, indeed.

Soon, she appeared before him, a look of resignation setting her features in place. He smiled at her in appreciation.

"It appears quiet right now. Why don't you take this chance for rest?" He gestured vaguely, feeling the absurdity of offering her rest in her own home. Despite her sense of readiness, he could detect the fatigue that emanated from her. She needed rest. Her powers demanded it.

"Are... are you sure?" She asked with trepidation, not wanting to appear too eager to close her weary eyes.

"Of course. I'll stand watch. Rest," he kept his voice low.

One of his hands ached to caress her face, but he resisted. Now was not the time. An idle moment passed between them where she seemed to wait for something more. He gave her none, so she nodded resolutely and settled, fully clothed on the small guest bed, the provisions she had packed standing nearby.

Evair tried not to get too transfixed in watching her sleep. It was not seemly, nor was it wise, considering the Dragon hunters were likely nearby. But the rise and fall of her chest, the way her eyelashes danced with the movements of her dreams threatened to steal his attention.

Resolutely, he turned away and forced himself to keep his eyes pointed outward, searching for any signs of movement. Some hours passed. The moon loitered with Evair for some time but then moved its lazy way out of his sight. He estimated it was nearing two or three in the morning.

His energy did not flag. He was happy to acknowledge. All of his ligaments, tendons and muscles stood in a state of relaxed readiness. It had been some time since he was planted in place, awaiting ambush. He was certain it would happen soon.

Minutes crawled past. Penelope's breathing remained steady and even. Evair let himself be soothed by it, let himself be steeled by it. He *would* protect her. That he knew.

Just then, at the edge of his hearing, he heard a distinct clicking sound. Like a falcon, he searched the area outside the window. Nothing. But the clicking sound persisted. Craning his neck, he tried to see past the periphery of the window… Still nothing.

Click. Click. Click. The rhythm and intensity increased. They were near, he was certain.

He was on the verge of leaving the room (something he was loath to do) when he caught a glimpse of movement. It appeared something or someone was trying to scale a window just down the side of the house, one that would lead into the bedroom at the end of the hall.

Whoever they were, they were clad in black, possibly wearing some sort of spiked boots to aid them in climbing the house. Evair was certain they were not alone. No sensible Dragon hunter would travel solo.

It was time to leave. Evair hated the idea with all his being, but he did not wish to confront Dragon slayers here. There was too much at stake, not the least of which was the fact that here they would be dangerously outnumbered.

Waking her as quietly as he dared, her eyes flew open. He merely nodded, and she arose, grabbing the pack. She joined him at the window, a rope already being lowered by him to the ground. They had been prescient indeed.

Within moments, their feet connected with the soft earth outside her home. Stealthily, they began to pick their way toward the street, hoping to clear the village and seek safety elsewhere.

At least that was the plan.

Crouching low, they cut diagonally across the lawn, keeping to the shadows. They had to clear at least half a league from the house to the place where Penelope's metal beast awaited them. From there, they intended to leave the town behind.

Snaking a path to avoid the glow from the upright lights that seemed to burn with a power Evair had not quite fathomed yet. They crouched, facing an open expanse of the street that was remarkably well lit for this time of the morning.

Communicating without speaking, Evair nodded at Penelope in a *go first* gesture. She nodded her understanding and launched across the open space, Evair close behind. Penelope was within striking distance of the shadows on the other side when an arrow zipped into her path like an unwelcome beacon.

Instantly, she drew back, Evair almost slamming into her. Throwing his arm around her shoulder, they hurled themselves into the shadows, landing crudely as more arrows rained around them. Still crouched, they pressed their bodies against the wall of a building. The darkness afforded them some degree of protection, and for a moment, the barrage ceased.

"We've been spotted," Penelope breathed, rubbing her elbow from the impact.

"I would tend to agree," Evair muttered coolly,

his eyes scanning the area around them, looking for the archers.

"We'll have to run... fast, jumping from shadow to shadow. We can't run to the car directly, it's too much in view. We'll have to zig-zag. Follow me," she said, as her body prepared to sprint.

He stopped her with a touch to her arm.

"Keep your eyes ahead. I'll watch the skies," he said. She began to protest, but he raised his hand in reply. He *would* be her shield; they both knew they should not use her magic unless absolutely necessary. Reluctantly, she agreed.

Within seconds, her body was in motion, Evair not far behind. Were they not being pursued by bloodthirsty killers, he would have admired this human witch's form and speed.

Another time, perhaps.

Muffled shouts soon echoed around them. They were surrounded, it seemed, although Evair could not pinpoint their vantage points. Stray arrows began to rain down again, and the clomp of feet drew near.

Evair dropped his head like a stallion as he charged forward, echoing Penelope's jagged egress through the streets of Whisper Falls.

Rage, pure and hot, bubbled within him. But he

would not allow it to overtake his reason. Like the forger's hammer, he hoped to sculpt the white-hot embers that torched within him into the power he needed to shift to his Dragon form.

Despite his efforts, which were herculean given that he was racing at top speed behind a witch running serpentine through an infested human encampment, he remained stubbornly a human.

A nagging thought beckoned at him: he could only shift if Penelope was hurt in some way. That was how he had shifted before. But this thought angered and appalled him, and he refused to entertain it.

There has to be another way.

Penelope continued darting and dancing from shadow to shadow, the blur of buildings and storefronts whizzing past. Arrows and other projectiles crashed in their path, and the sounds of boots increased. Miraculously, Penelope was adept and agile enough to avoid everything thrown in their path.

"There... up ahead... " She breathed, her hair streaming out from behind her. Evair could see the metal beast waiting patiently in the tiny space allotted to it some distance ahead. The Dragon slayers had not thought to disable it.

If only I could shift, we would have no need for this human claptrap.

Just then, a bottle containing some sort of flame burst in the small space between Penelope and Evair. At once, clouds of noxious vapor exploded around them, causing them to momentarily separate.

He could no longer see Penelope. He could hear her gasps for air but could not find her. In the confusion, Evair began to panic. Not at the potential for bodily harm to himself, but at the thought of losing her.

She was, he knew, connected to his powers in some way. He was willing to admit she was connected in a monumental bond, but he could not fathom how deep.

Sputtering and choking, he scrambled forward, his arms outstretched when finally, his fingers brushed against fabric.

"Penelope!" He gagged, his fingers tearing at the fabric.

She was his connection to this world. She had ensured his survival. Perhaps, just *perhaps,* she was his mate. The thought entered squarely in his mind just as he felt her fingers intertwine with his.

"Evair!" She choked, her arms crawling up to his chest in relief.

Just as his name escaped her lips, Evair felt the disorienting sensation he had so longed for.

He had shifted. He was a Dragon once more.

20
PENELOPE

Panic turned to elation as Penelope felt Evair's fingers cease their grip on her shirt. She sensed they were no longer fingers but talons connected to his powerful feet. Dragon feet.

Still, she could not see him. The smoke bomb occluded her vision, choked her mouth and lungs. Even if she wanted to cast a spell, she lacked the ability to speak, concentrate, or even see her own two hands in front of her. All were crucial to a successful spell cast.

His transformation was a welcome development, but she instantly felt another constriction in her chest... fear. He was now a large target, and they could be ambushed. But his strength, agility, and powers were a great asset when it seemed that the Dragon slayers surrounded them at every turn.

They had been near her car when the smoke bomb was deployed. All her focus had been on getting to it without being injured or worse. Now, she halted her movements. The car was no longer needed.

A great howl shattered the early morning air. Penelope's hands clamped over her ears as Evair howled his anger and frustration at the town of Whisper Falls. She felt the street beneath her shake with his rage.

"Climb on." His quiet words stunned her after his outburst. By now, the smoke had begun to clear, leaving them exposed, but at least she could see his luminescent skin and magnificent features glint in the eerie light.

Debris and arrows began to rain down again, especially now that they were so visible. As long as they stayed in this spot, they were asking to be killed.

Evair bent one shoulder to the ground, and Penelope scrambled up to nestle behind his head. Despite the chaos around them, she marveled at the realization that the creature she now sat upon was only too recently entwined in her arms... in an entirely different form.

Dismissing the thought, she grappled his taut neck muscles as his whole body leapt from the ground like a scaly Harrier jump jet. Her insides lurched downward from the sudden change in direction.

Together, they ascended several feet above the buildings that they had used as shelter just moments ago. The change in topography was dizzying, and Penelope had to close her eyes momentarily. Evair seemed to suffer no such disorientation as he sought out an air current by which to glide while scouring the landscape below.

When she was able, Penelope opened her eyes. If the streets themselves had been deserted, the rooftops were a different story. Like cockroaches that scatter when the light is turned on, they were littered with Dragon slayers, who scuttled and regrouped now that Evair was above them.

Hordes of supplies and weapons could be seen near the edges of the roofs, all part of the arsenal that had been hurled at them. Through the rush of wind and the beating of his wings, Penelope could hear muffled shouts from below as they struggled to regroup.

"What's the plan?" Penelope shouted. She felt a little helpless up here in the air, although she was glad to be off the ground.

"We find the leader. Nestor. We eliminate him, and the rest will scatter." Evair's voice was hard and flinty. Penelope felt a flutter of fear, exhilaration, and excitement ripple through her. She would not want to be on the receiving end of Evair's wrath.

Evair began to survey the world below him in ever widening circles, his eyes darting methodically over the activity below. Penelope did the same from her limited perch, scouring the movement below for any telltale signs of Nestor.

After what seemed like an eternity, Evair swooped low over a nondescript building that lay nestled on the edge of town. Used by the village as a storage facility for rock salt and other items. It had a large sloping roof and very little lighting.

A small group of Dragon slayers was congregated at the bottom of the roof's slope, their shapes poised as they looked above. It seemed like they had been waiting for Evair to arrive.

Penelope was certain Nestor was among them. Unlike the other scattered groups they had encountered, this one seemed more in tune, more synchronized.

"There. He's there," Evair breathed. Penelope simply patted his neck in agreement.

Now what?

The sloping roof put them at a disadvantage. The hunters below could easily jump to the ground and scatter, and the slope made Evair's ability to access them trickier. Plus, Penelope did not want a bloodbath. Nestor had to be contained, that was certain, but she did not want to wipe out an entire group of people... even if they were loathsome thugs.

Evair, she feared, would have no such scruples. Penelope had to find a middle ground somewhere.

"We need to separate him from the group. Let me use some magic. If we can get close enough, I can isolate him and bring him to us," she proposed, hoping her calm demeanor would persuade him.

"How do you propose we do that?" She could not tell by his tone if he was in the mood for listening or if he was just humoring her. Deciding she did not have time to think about it, she continued.

"Follow the slope of the roof. Head straight for them. Some will scatter just at that. Nestor likely won't. When we're in range, I can cast a levitation spell and bring him to us."

"And after that?"

"You can do what you wish with him."

Three tense seconds of silence followed. Penelope held her breath.

"I consent," he replied, and Penelope exhaled in relief. She was glad they had a plan. And none too soon, it seemed, as the air around them suddenly became alive with arrows once more. They were aiming for the delicate membranes of Evair's wings, knowing it could tear them from the sky. They had to act quickly.

Evair tucked his wings closer to his body, and Penelope had the distinct feeling it was in her best interest to hang on even tighter to his neck. Soaring upwards, he easily outpaced the arrows that came remarkably close.

Evair pitched upward, pulling away from the ground as if gravity had no hold on them anymore. In the next instant, there was a moment of stillness, like all the air had been sucked from the world, and they lay suspended between sound and silence, motion and stasis. Then, his head turned downward, and the air began to tear past them, an acceleration Penelope had never before experienced.

It took everything in her power, not to blackout. She *had* to get ready to cast the spell. They only had one chance.

The ground zoomed to meet them at an alarming pace. Evair began to slant his body in relation to the roof that was rapidly coming into view. Penelope could practically see the rivets that held it onto the structure below.

As predicted, the group that surrounded Nestor began to scatter at their approach. The arrows ceased their tumult, and Penelope could hear shouts of fury emit from Nestor's open mouth.

Just a bit closer...

Reluctantly, she pulled her hands from Evair's neck, gripping him ever tighter with her legs. She needed her hands to cast the spell.

Evair had aligned himself with the slope of the roof and was heading towards it, like a ski jumper. She closed her eyes and began to whisper the spidery Latin that would engulf Nestor... if she cast it at exactly the right moment.

Just a touch closer...

Now. Opening her eyes, she flung her hands

away from herself as the last word escaped her lips. An angry orange ball erupted from them, and she saw the remaining stalwarts of his crew flee in terror. Nestor, however, held his ground, his eyes widening as the ball descended and engulfed him.

He would feel no pain, Penelope knew. But she could not speak for his fear. And she knew that pain was not far behind if Evair had his way.

Evair, meanwhile, having seen the orange ball engulf Nestor, pulled up just as the slope leveled off, and they plateaued in the air.

Penelope pulled her hands sharply to her chest, which caused the bubble to snap to attention. Nestor was now tethered to her, and he was rapidly rising in the air until he was a floating prisoner before Evair's hungry gaze.

Another moment of stillness and silence descended. Nestor raised his hands, within the bubble, in a gesture of supplication. His arrows, smoke bombs, and slavish followers could do nothing for him now.

"He's all yours," Penelope whispered. She kept her hands still, holding the bubble intact.

"I am most pleased," Evair responded. She felt his attention, white-hot and menacingly deliberate, turn to the terrified human trapped before him.

"Please... please," Nestor could be heard within, his voice oddly distended and frantic.

"You have not earned the right to speak. Not anymore. You are the worst of your kind. And your antics are over. I will make sure of that," Evair barely spoke above a whisper, which seemed all the more frightening... even to Penelope.

"I'm sure we can come to some sort of arrangement..."

"You lost that privilege long ago. Enough," Evair replied. He began to draw his lips together tightly.

Nestor began to protest wildly and maniacally, sensing his end was near. With all her might, Penelope wanted to close her eyes against whatever came next, but she knew she needed to maintain the spell. Gulping, she steeled herself.

Evair continued to draw in air. Penelope was certain that any moment, he would release his breath, and a torrent of wind would toss Nestor to pieces.

That is not what happened. Evair continued to draw in his breath, and Penelope saw Nestor reach up to grab at his throat. Like a fish out of water, he began to thrash and buck. Evair was *sucking* the air out of the bubble.

Penelope's hands clenched as she witnessed Nestor's writhing death throes. Evair continued to draw in air, ensuring that not one particle of oxygen remained.

Several excruciating moments later, Nestor's arms dropped limply, and his head soon followed. Although he remained suspended in the bubble, it was clear he was held up only by Penelope's magic.

Evair ceased drawing in the air. He hovered quietly, assessing Nestor carefully, looking for any signs of life.

Penelope knew, deep within her bones, there was none to be found. Nestor was well and truly gone.

And, as predicted, she saw scatters of his followers flee, leaving behind their weapons and equipment.

"Let's lower him down," she said quietly. Despite his actions and his grisly death, Penelope could not condone simply dropping his corpse to the ground below.

Evair grunted in reply, and together, they maneuvered the bubble to a flat roof close by. Evair landed, his talons digging deep into the roof tiles. Penelope lowered her hands, and the bubble descended, finally dissipating as Nestor's body crumpled.

"Give me a minute," she told Evair, sliding down his shoulder and to the roof. Approaching slowly, she searched Nestor's body for any signs of movement or breathing. He was still as a stone.

Muttering a silent prayer such as one gives a vanquished foe, Penelope rearranged Nestor so that he appeared to be sleeping. While he was a monster, she still believed he was worthy of respect... even in death.

As she did so, she checked his pockets. She found a cell phone in his front pocket, the screen illuminated with messages. All to and from concerned and increasingly frantic followers.

She scrolled quickly through them, fear and concern bubbling up within her. Evair must have sensed it because he stepped close to her.

"What is it? Does that glowing machine tell you anything?"

"I think so. His last messages are broken up. He seemed to be sending messages right up until the end," she squinted, trying to piece the messages together.

"And...?"

"He told his followers to go to plan B."

"And what is that?" Concern crept into Evair's voice.

"They are to look for another Dragon. One named Aelon."

Penelope heard Evair gasp... a small intake of breath.

"Do you know that name?" She almost didn't want to hear the answer.

"We must leave," was all he said.

"Tell me."

"Aelon is my brother. The youngest. We must go. Now."

Penelope gave Nestor's body one more look. All feelings of pity for him had receded.

21
EVAIR

The glory of his Dragon shape wreathed Evair in power. Fury was rising in his blood, not yet quelled... even after slaughtering Nestor.

"We must move quickly," Evair said. "We don't know how much of a start they have."

"The last messages weren't that long ago," Penny said, looking into the bright screen of the small device. Evair wasn't entirely sure how it worked, but if they were communicating recently, then the hunters were probably moving on his brother right now.

"How will we find him?" asked Penny. "There are some clues here about the mountain and ridge, but it could take a long time to figure out exactly where he is."

"There will be yarrow growing," said Evair. "I also believe that I will be able to home in on him by instinct. I know where he is likely to lie, and perhaps, I will be able to smell him or see signs of him."

"Okay," Penny looked at him, concern crossing her features. "We can't exactly drive... Unless you can shift at will now?" her eyes were wide and hopeful, but Evair only shook his long Dragon head at her.

"No, I do not feel fluid at all. It is well, though. You can ride me, and we will travel much faster."

"Ride you again?" she asked softly. She seemed just a bit nervous now that they weren't fighting for their lives.

"Yes," Evair said, a little impatiently. He leaned down, stretching out his wing, so his shoulder slid towards the ground. Penny took a few steps closer, stroking his smooth, white scales as they reflected the light back to her in a stunning shimmer of blue, green, and amethyst.

Evair shivered as her hand moved across his flesh. Her skin was impossibly smooth against the hard scales and felt very warm. She caressed him gently as if she were reassuring a horse, sidling up to him to grab the spines at the base of his neck.

He leaned down even further as she pulled herself up, kicking with one leg to leap up and throw herself bodily against him. Evair tried to stay steady as she wriggled into place, but when her legs clamped around his shoulders, he felt a warm thrill run through him.

For a moment, heat flushed through his every cell. If a Dragon could blush, he certainly would have. Her knees dug into him while her silky thighs rubbed up and down as she made herself comfortable. Her hands gripped his neck spines, and she reached down to give him a gentle pat.

He shivered again, and Penny scratched his neck gently.

"Are you okay, Evair?"

"Yes, I am well," he snapped. He turned towards the mountains, rearing back on his hind legs and flapping his wings. He stayed in that position for a few seconds, like a bird testing the breeze, mostly making sure that Penny was secure.

It seemed as if the flat base of his neck was designed for her to sit in. Her legs hung down in front of his wings and gripped firmly above his shoulders. He shifted his weight several times to make sure she was secure, then launched from the ground, powering up into the sky with hard beats of his wings.

He felt Penny slide back and forth as he thrust upwards, keeping herself secure with her hands and knees. The wind lifted under his wings, and he caught a strong gust that took him high in only a few seconds. He focused on the peaks, using small economic movements to adjust his path.

He didn't want to unseat or tire Penny with too many aerial acrobatics. The less he flapped his wings, the less likely she would be to fall off. He had never flown so carefully in his long life.

The feel of her body moving against his continued to make heat grow in his blood, distracting him from the fury he felt at the Dragon hunters. For the briefest of moments, he closed his eyes and enjoyed the feel of her body against his. She slid gently, back and forth, and Evair had to open his eyes and focus on flying again simply to take his mind off which parts of her were touching him.

"Head that way," Penny shouted against the wind. She pointed at the lower peaks, just under the shadow of a much higher mountain. Evair nodded. It was a likely place for his brother to hide.

They spiraled above the peak, Evair feeling the thrill of hope as he spotted yarrow growing in tufts across the summit. The winds were rough here, so close to the highest peak, and he had to adjust his descent to float slowly into the lee of the mountain.

Penny's hands gripped him twice as hard as he made his final turn and landed as gently as he could on his hind legs. He tried to absorb the shock so Penny wouldn't fall, but she turned to the side and slid down his shoulder with ease, using the momentum to help her get down smoothly.

Evair shook himself all over, groaning just a little as his large body rattled out the tension of the flight. When he opened his eyes, Penny was watching him with an amused look on her face.

"What?" he asked, trying not to sound defensive.

"You just looked a little bit like a horse getting up from a roll."

Evair made a grunt of disapproval and immediately realized that was exactly what a horse would do. He frowned, hoping it wasn't a horse-like expression, and headed for the cave entrance.

It was a large cleft in the rock, easily big enough to admit a Dragon. Evair sat up on his hind legs to examine the runes printed across the top of the entrance.

"Draconic runes," he said. Penny looked up curiously.

"May I see?" she asked. He lifted her on his front claw, a little awkwardly. She finally settled in his palm, and he was able to bring her close to the rock face.

"They are beautiful. What do they mean?"

"Here lies a fierce prince, a powerful Dragon. Any who disturb his resting place will bear the wrath of his fury, should they survive the traps set to catch the unwary and those of no honor."

"Traps?" Penny asked as he set her down. "What about traps?"

Evair shrugged. "It takes some doing to defend your cave in this way. He may have had humans build it around him, or he built the traps when he was on his way in, sealing the tunnel behind him."

"That's fascinating, but I was more asking, what kind of traps?"

"Oh. Of that, I have no idea. It could be

anything. Falling blocks, suddenly slamming doors, pits, spikes, rolling rocks..."

"Okay, okay," Penny waved a hand. "I get the picture. We should have brought Indiana Jones or Lara Croft."

"Excuse me?" Evair asked, mystified. "Are these people Dragon experts?" he was genuinely curious if such a thing existed in this modern age. Penny laughed.

"No. They raid tombs for treasure and adventure, collecting artifacts."

"Extraordinary," Evair said as they entered the doorway. "Can they be found and employed by me to search out others of my kind? I have ample funds."

Penny giggled. "They are fictional characters, Evair."

He frowned. "So how, exactly, are they supposed to help us?"

Penny sighed, sounding as if she were entering her doom. Evair was getting sick of that sound just as he was getting sick of feeling a step behind.

"If you do not wish me to misunderstand, then speak plainly," he snapped. She looked up at him sharply, her green eyes gleaming in the shadows of the cave mouth.

"I apologize, Evair. I'm not trying to make fun of you. Pop culture references are just a casual form of conversation these days. I really do forget that you won't understand the reference."

Evair put in a decent effort to pull his Dragon features into a thoughtful frown. Penny was walking just ahead, running her hand across the cold stone, sensing its properties.

"Then you must promise to show me these characters, so I can understand," he said. Penny nodded.

"You got it, big guy. Binge session is penciled in for the future. Snacks, and shadows, and snuggling on the couch."

She immediately blushed and looked up at him bashfully, but he just nodded, growling a little in his throat. He leaned down and pressed his head against her body, and she stroked his nose.

"I have caught snatches of this modern 'lingo'," he said carefully. "I believe what you refer to is called Netflix and chill?"

Penny laughed, patting his nose again. "Exactly. Good catch, Evair."

"Catch?"

"Oh lord," she muttered. "What a minefield."

"There are mines too?" he snapped, in alarm.

"Evair!" she allowed her voice to rise, just a little. "Since I don't have time to give you full and complete explanations right now, can you just put things aside in your mind for us to talk about later? I'm trying to control my speech for you as best I can."

"Alright," he muttered grumpily. "Let us continue. The place seems deserted. Perhaps we have come in time."

"No," Penny whispered, bending over. She picked up a crushed cigarette butt, still faintly warm. "They are here. Well, someone is, and they aren't far ahead."

"Then proceed," he said, getting anxious. "My brother will be helpless if he is in a deep sleep. We must catch up."

"Okay," Penny headed into the dark hallway. "I am sensing with my instincts as well as my magic. Let me know if you feel anything."

"I will," Evair muttered. He did not like the feel of this place. Even though he had felt like burying himself several times since his awakening, he now found he didn't want to get trapped under the mountain. There was little room for fighting or escape, and he knew these Dragon hunters were determined, skilled, and vicious.

He watched Penny walking slowly ahead of him, knowing that he couldn't let anything happen to her. He could deny that she was his mate all he wanted, but there was clearly a connection there that he could not ignore.

22
PENELOPE

They advanced into the shadows. It became so dark that Penny literally couldn't see even an inch in front of her face, and she made a small ball of silver light to float just in front of them to light the way.

The hallway was getting narrower already, and Penny didn't know how far Evair would be able to travel into the tunnels. As much as she wanted him with her, she wasn't keen to have him so close to the Dragon hunters. Penny wasn't exactly frightened, but she was feeling high anxiety.

Penny wanted to help Evair find his brother, and she definitely wanted to make sure they stopped the Dragon hunters. Now that she knew that Dragons were real, she certainly wasn't going to let anything happen to them. These feelings tangled in her emotions concerning Evair himself, though.

Penny wanted to just fly away with him, disappear to somewhere safe where they could curl up and tell each other endless stories. She wanted to keep him from harm. Constantly, Penny fought with herself, trying to convince her heart that he was a friend, someone she wanted to help and nothing more.

With every step, her heart beat in time with her feet, rebelling against common sense. Penny couldn't deny the affection that was growing in her, the connection she felt to him. Several times she almost reached out to touch him casually, reminding herself at the last second that the relationship was not yet that intimate.

It feels like it is, she thought. It felt like they had known each other from the beginning of time all the way to its end. A perspective that went in both directions. It was an unusual feeling, but it also felt perfectly natural.

Penny berated herself for not focusing on the task at hand and turned her attention back to the shadowy corridor. There was the sound of water dripping somewhere deep in the cavern, making a gentle echo. She kept her fingertips against the cool stone wall, reaching out with her senses for any changes to the air.

"I smell blood," Evair said, pausing. Penny stopped too, feeling danger ahead more than smelling it.

"Higher," she whispered to her magic orb. It swelled and rose to the ceiling, revealing a long stretch of hallway that was completely straight and narrow. There was a lumpy figure on the ground not far ahead. Penny focused on it, gasping.

"It's a body!" she exclaimed, wincing as her voice rang off the stone, echoing down and up the chamber. Evair sniffed the air and took a step forward, his claws clicking on the floor.

Penny took deep breaths, looking up at the ceiling and carefully examining the walls. Not far ahead of her, she saw a dark shape jutting out of the wall. With a whisper, she directed her light towards it.

"Look, Evair," she whispered. It was a long, thick blade that was stuck in the rock, jammed there by a heavy ax.

"Ah," he said, examining it. "The blade sweeps out through this crack, quite swiftly, I imagine. An old gravity and pulley system, much more effective than your modern machinery. Reliable too, for hundreds of years. It's probably activated by a trigger in the floor."

Penny stepped forward gingerly. "How will we know where it is?" she asked.

"It doesn't matter," he said. "The ax is blocking it, so the blade is caught in its track. One of these hunters has impeccable reflexes and impressive strength. He must have drawn his weapon right before the other guy went down."

"Sent him ahead as bait, more likely," she muttered. Evair nodded.

"That is also a possibility."

"Okay," she took a few steps forward, still touching the wall as she moved. When she approached the body, she bent to touch him on the shoulder, avoiding his headless neck.

"Still warm," she whispered. Evair nodded.

"His blood has not finished draining. He has not been here long."

"We need to keep moving," she whispered. Penny was worried for Evair as the corridor narrowed. The further in they were, the more vulnerable he became. They kept moving, the little glowing ball of light bobbing ahead of them as they went.

Ahead, the magic glow revealed a wide open foyer before an even narrower door. The edges of the wall were decorated in the draconian runes.

"What do these say?" she asked. Evair looked them over.

"It reveals that four sealings protect the Dragon within. We have passed the first, yet there are three more to go. The next seal has a symbol of a square spiral."

"Also called a maze," whispered Penny. Evair nodded.

"I have to check it out," she said, heading for the doorway. Evair reached out, pulling her back.

"No," he said, "you can't go alone."

"I'm just going to take a quick look, then we'll decide what to do," she answered. He didn't look happy about it, but he released her so she could head for the doorway. It was very small, smaller than the door to her house, but not so small she had to crouch. If Evair was very careful and patient, he could probably fit through, but with extreme difficulty. She ran her fingers along the wall, her senses on fire. She followed her magic light to the end of the short corridor and sent the light up high so it could show her the layout of the room.

In front of her, the room opened out into a circular space. Ahead was a narrow doorway. The sound of stone scraping could be heard, very faintly. She took a few more steps forward, wary of any more blades, and peeked through the door.

Impossible hallways wound away from it, with small doors opening and closing up and down each corridor. It was probably far too small for Evair to fit through, and she was disappointed that she would have to go alone, as well as relieved he wouldn't have to risk getting trapped deeper in the mountain.

She hurried back to Evair, her magic light following her. He was sitting in the corner, wrapped in his wings with his tail tucked around his body.

"What did you find?" he asked, sitting up.

"It's a maze," she said. "A very twisty one. I don't think you'll fit, Evair."

He looked between her and the small doorway.

"I fear you are right, Penelope," he said softly. "We must abandon the mission and attempt to enter another way."

Penny shook her head, not sure that she'd heard correctly.

"What are you talking about?"

"You can't go alone, Penny."

She straightened up to her full height, crossing her arms tightly across her chest.

"I have a few thousand clever retorts running through my mind right now, but all of them involve modern pop culture references regarding equal rights. Since I'd risk insulting you, I won't be a smartass about it, but basically, that is bullshit."

"Excuse me?" Evair said, mystified. Penny frowned at him.

"It's so sweet that you feel you need to protect me, but…"

"I don't intend for it to be sweet or not," Evair snapped, interrupting. "You are not going alone. That is final."

Penny's eyebrows rose slowly as if her surprise was taking time to register.

"Evair, you don't give modern women orders, okay?"

"But it's dangerous, and you…"

"I am a perfectly capable human being!" she snapped. "I can take care of myself, thank you very much. I will go on, and you can wait here."

"Wait here?" he spluttered, his Dragon face looking ridiculous in a state of indignance. Penny nodded firmly, walking across the cave to touch his nose.

"I'll be alright, Evair."

"I don't know that, and neither do you," he muttered sullenly.

"Don't you trust me?" she asked. His big, dark eyes met hers, and she stared him down.

"I don't trust anything else," he hissed. "You don't know what you're walking into!"

She shrugged. "I don't need to be protected, Evair. Maybe it's about time you trusted someone to help you, instead."

He spluttered, trying to protest. She stroked his nose again then headed back to the doorway where her magic light was waiting for her.

"This thing looks incredible," she said, grinning. "Even if I didn't have to do this, I'd still want to. You should see it. I think a person could get lost in here for years."

"That is exactly my point," Evair muttered, arranging himself on the ground again. Penny almost made a snappy remark, but instead, she just smiled. They looked into each other's eyes, neither wanting to say goodbye.

Penny took a deep breath and quickly headed through the doorway, hurrying through the foyer to the door to the maze. The magic light hung above her head as she paused, wondering if she should go right or left. The corridor was narrow, and she could see openings in both directions.

She sent out a trickle of magic, sensing that she should head left. Immediately that felt wrong, so she turned back around, only to pause as anxiety gripped her once again.

Well, this is just great, she thought. *My instincts have gone haywire. How the hell am I supposed to navigate?*

She looked up for her glowing orb, but it was high above her now, angling itself above the walls of the maze, which were at least fifteen feet tall and disappearing into shadow. Starting to panic, Penny turned around and ran her hand along the wall, searching for the way out so she could orient herself and maybe even run back to Evair.

Her stomach started to drop out as she ran along.

There is no opening in this wall!

The entrance was sealed. There was no way to get out.

Except to solve the maze.

23
EVAIR

When Evair saw Penny disappear into the maze, he knew he couldn't let her go alone. The edges of the cave felt like they were pressing in on him, and he knew if they met up with the Dragon hunters, he would be far too vulnerable, but none of that mattered now.

The only thing that mattered was Penny.

He got up and slithered through the small hallway, coming out on the other side to a wide room. Ahead of it was the entrance to the maze. It looked like solid rock, and he wondered how she had gotten in.

He approached the wall, looking up and down for a possible entrance. He tried flying up as best he could in the enclosed area but couldn't open his wings far enough. He knew that the area had to have a roof even if he couldn't see it in the dark. The maze would be no good if anyone could fly over the walls.

He pressed his claws to the rock and felt a slight vibration. He stepped away quickly as the wall began to rumble. An opening appeared, very briefly, and he slipped through.

"Evair!" Penny yelled, jogging up to him. "Where did you come from? I thought you couldn't fit through."

"I managed it," he said, trying to stand up so that he could walk along the passage. It felt horribly cramped. No matter which way he turned, some part of him got caught in the slender halls.

A cage.

He shook off the thought and focused on Penny. She was looking up at him with wide, green eyes, a smile of pleasure lighting her face. His heart jumped a few beats in his chest, making him dizzy. He gently lowered his nose to her, and she wrapped her arms around his face.

"Never leave me," her whisper was so soft, he barely heard it. He could feel her heart pounding against his forehead and hear the rush of her breathing.

"I won't," he whispered. Her arms tightened on him for a few seconds before she let go. He saw her straighten her shoulders and look down the hall, ready to continue.

"Which way?" he asked, genuinely confused. Even though the floor was level and still, he felt like he was spinning. His sense of direction was completely destroyed in this place.

"I'm still trying to figure that out," she said, taking a few steps down the hall. "I didn't even realize the doors were moving until you came through."

"Yes, it looked like a solid wall from the outside, too."

"Let's see..." Penny walked down the hall a bit, pausing by an opening in the rock. She closed her eyes briefly and touched the wall before hurrying through. Evair followed her, but it was tricky to move through the doorway and get into the hallway on the other side.

"Come this way," she said eagerly. She jogged up the hall, heading for a doorway on her right this time. Evair followed as fast as he could, hearing the thunk of rock nearby as doors opened and closed.

Penny kept moving, waving him forward. Evair was getting tired of turning on himself like a snake to navigate the narrow openings, as well as bruising his wings on the rock as he made the tight turns, but he did not complain.

"Ah-ha!" Penny announced as they turned into the next hallway in a flourish. Evair looked around, not sure what he was supposed to be seeing.

"What is it?"

"We're back at the original starting point. Wait a second."

He watched where she did and was astonished to see the wall open, the stone scraping as the pieces moved slowly apart. He spied the large, domed space of the room where they had entered the maze.

"Okay, you got us back to the start," he said skeptically, "But how do we get to the middle?"

She laughed, shaking out her hair. She picked up a loose rock from the edge of the hallway and drew a couple of circles on the ground with the small, chalky piece of stone.

"I'm not sure how many rings there are, not yet," she said. "But the walls are on a rotating spindle. They move constantly, but there has to be regularity to it. It's not random."

It all became clear to Evair very suddenly as he watched her draw out the circle of rings, playing with possible locations of openings.

"So, if you run wildly down the hallways, you would never find the center," he said, amused. "But if you stay put and wait for the openings to come to you, then you could basically walk in a straight line from the entrance to the center."

"Smart Dragon," Penny said, leaning forward and grabbing his snout to plant a kiss between his nostrils. He blinked, leaning forward into her caress, only to feel suddenly self-conscious. He could tell by her immediate reaction that she did, too, and both of them jumped back and looked away.

"Well, then," Evair said gruffly. "You lead the way."

Penny nodded, looking at the wall and not at Evair. As the opening she was looking for arrived and slid into place, she ushered him through. They did this several more times, barely moving up or down the corridor each time.

"What is that sound?" Evair asked, tilting his

head from side to side. He peered into the shadows, craning his neck.

"The whispering?" Penny asked. He nodded.

"I don't know," she said. "It's just on the edge of hearing... It chatters and hisses."

"Yes," Evair said. "Voices not corporeal, and yet they can speak."

"Enough," Penny said harshly. "The deep shadows are quite enough. I don't want to think about how many nightmare creatures are out there that I always believed were imaginary but are, in fact, real."

"Well, actually..." he began.

"No!" she snapped. "Tell me all about ethereal cave dwellers later. After we get out of here."

"So, I shall," he said. "I must find some decent brandy to share with you. Are there any monasteries nearby?"

"Monasteries?" she asked, mystified. He looked at her with the same amount of surprise.

"Monks are secluded and live in the perfect conditions for distilling brandy," he said, a little defensively.

"You can't just have a nice bottle of wine?"

"Uuk," Evair shook his head, spitting. "I would

never touch such swill. Warm weather alcohol. Not nearly potent enough for me."

"Duly noted," Penny laughed. "Only the top shelf for you."

"Liquor should be stored at the bottom of the cupboard, far in the back. Hot air rises, you know."

"I do," Penny said, rolling her eyes. Evair realized it was one of her modern day jokes but decided not to pursue it. He was starting to find that look on her face kind of cute and began to think of ways he could purposely misunderstand in an attempt to see it more often.

"Whoa," she said, pausing. In a very slender crack in the wall, the body of a woman was crushed. She wore black fatigues and was well armored.

"One of the hunters," Evair sniffed, displeased. "I guess she didn't solve the maze."

"No," Penny agreed. "It's interesting though, we haven't seen a single skeleton. That means no one has ever come through here, ever. Your brother picked a good hiding place."

"Well," Evair agreed, "It reeks of paranoia. He must have been planning his long sleep for some time to go to this much trouble."

"What did you do?" she asked, curious.

"Oh, I just got tired and fed up. Decided to disappear. I made a little earthquake to bury myself."

Penny started laughing, covering her mouth. He gazed at her curiously.

"I'm sorry," she said. "I just had an image of you lying in the dirt scuffing your feet and wings like a chicken having a dust bath."

Evair was about to be offended when the image suddenly struck him in full force, and he found himself laughing too. They were still laughing as they hurried through the gap in the wall. Penny winced as it slammed shut, pulverizing the hunter's body even more.

"Not far to go now," she said. "I think the movements get faster towards the center, but there are fewer doors."

"Hmm. I shall have to take your word for it. I'm quite lost right now."

Penny put a hand on his shoulder to hold him in place while the opening came around. She wouldn't let him go through until the circle had come around at least three times.

"Some openings are larger than others," she said. "I wanted to make sure you had as much room as possible."

He nodded, about to say something sweet, when he heard the sound of weapons being drawn. Then, he could smell humans, quite a few of them.

"They are close."

"Probably through the next opening," she whispered. They watched the wall move past several times, seeing nothing on the other side but a tall stone dais in the middle of a ring of stone. They had no choice but to go through.

Penny grabbed Evair's neck spines and rushed through the door by his side. They both whirled, watching the opening close behind them. Evair reared back on his hind legs, opening his wings as he turned around. Penny watched the shadows, thinking at first that they were alone.

Then an arrow whistled out of the dark, punching through Evair's wing. He roared in anger and pain, whirling to face the attack. Penny saw the hunters, five of them, moving swiftly from the shadows around the central pillar. She screamed, and Evair thought it was the worst sound he had ever heard.

She ran forward, trying to jump in front of Evair. He swept one claw out, taking her feet out from under her, so she stumbled. The next barrage of arrows came straight at him. He roared as they hit, puncturing his shoulders and chest with the fiery burn of Dragon's bane.

He saw Penny trying to get up, and he struggled to get in front of her. Maybe, if they had him, they would leave her alone. Suddenly, everything was clear to Evair for the first time in his very long life.

All that mattered was Penny. He didn't care about anything else. He would give his life to save her.

Evair roared and charged the hunters, praying that she would flee while he gave her time to escape.

24
PENELOPE

Penny felt the cold stone floor smack her in the side of the face as Evair tipped her over, letting her momentum carry her out of the line of fire. He leapt forward, roaring as he released a huge wave of strong, icy wind.

She tried to get up but was too dazed. The strength of Evair's power astonished her as the windstorm began to push her across the floor. One of the hunters was pinned to the wall, screaming as the wind crushed him. Others were crouched behind the stones that scattered around the rest of the room.

Penny gasped against the wind, trying to pull herself up. Evair roared, releasing even more power. She saw three of the hunters moving around behind the rocks, all of them managing to avoid the windstorm. When Penny looked back at Evair, he was faltering. That was when she noticed he had already been hit by quite a few arrows.

"No!" she screamed. To her horror, Evair charged the last three hunters, rushing at them and roaring.

They had dived for cover, and Evair went after them, raking with his claws and snapping with his strong jaws. Penny struggled to her feet, trying to look for a weapon. She realized even if she found one, she wouldn't be very good at using it. She stood up and ran to the edge of the room where Evair was trying to kill the Dragon hunters with claws and fangs.

She saw one leap out of his hiding place and try to flank Evair. She threw a bolt of power that knocked him off his feet, but she wasn't quick enough to bring him down. He fired an arrow into Evair's chest.

He staggered back, and Penny counted four arrows in him now, plus the wound in his wing. She didn't know exactly how long Dragon's bane took to work, but surely, he couldn't keep this up for much longer.

All the Dragon hunters were getting up now,

finding cover behind the low rock ledges. Evair let out another strong blast of wind, but all of them managed to gain cover. Penny could hear them shouting at each other. She willed her power and sent her magic out to help Evair, but immediately felt so weak she had to stop.

I've drawn on my power too much, and now it's turned on me! she thought. Headaches, weakness, fatigue, these had always been the price for using too much of her power. If she collapsed in here, they would both die for certain.

All five Dragon hunters moved from their positions at the same time. They fired their arrows from separate locations, and each one hit its target. With a horrible scream, Evair went down.

"No!" she screamed, racing across the room. Her heart was stuck in her throat, and her eyes were stinging. She had never been so afraid in her entire life.

She sank to the ground as she reached his head, cradling his nose so she could look into his eyes.

"Evair?" she whispered, desperate. He blinked slowly, every movement causing him pain.

"Leave me," he growled. "Go, run."

Then his eyes closed, rolling back into his head. She could still see his chest moving and feel his breath, but she knew he didn't have long. She stroked his nose gently, tears pouring down her cheeks.

Behind her, she heard the hunters approaching. They sounded pretty confident, and why shouldn't they? Penny wished she could turn around with her hands blazing with power and merge them with the rock walls like a badass movie witch, but that was beyond her strength. Hopeless tears continued to fall as their footsteps got closer and closer.

Would they kill me, too? she thought. Probably. They would hack Evair to pieces… right here and now. Would they kill her before they started carving up her lover? Her stomach lurched, and she slapped her hand across her mouth.

I cannot let this happen.

"Wait just a second!" she yelled, whirling around and jumping to her feet. "Stop right there!"

"Oh, yeah?" the tallest guy in the middle of the group leveled a gun at her head. He had put his bow away and was regarding her with some amusement.

"Why shouldn't I just kill you?" he sneered.

"You're lost, aren't you?" she asked softly. The

other hunters looked at Big Guy in alarm. He frowned, trying to scare her by getting even closer.

"Don't insult me," he hissed. She cocked her head and grinned.

"You really are lost, aren't you?"

"Shut the fuck up!"

"Listen," she said eagerly. "I can get you out of here. Obviously, you navigated to the center on your own, but you have no idea how to get out, do you?"

His eyes showed a brief flash of fear. He glanced around then back into Penny's face.

"Why would you help us?" he asked. She looked at Evair.

"Leave him. Don't hurt him anymore. Don't…" she tried to express in more detail what she didn't want to happen, but the words were too gruesome to say out loud.

"Just leave him," she said. "I'll take you out of the maze if you just leave him alone."

The guy glanced around her, watching Evair's breathing getting slower by the second. He laughed.

"He's about to die, anyway. What does it matter?"

"Just promise me you'll leave his body here, and I'll get you out of this maze."

The guy cocked his head, grinning. The other hunters watched the exchange curiously. Penny knew that the guy was probably thinking he could come back for Evair's bones after she led him out of here. Once he knew the way, there was nothing to stop him from killing her.

She didn't care. The only thing that mattered was getting the hunters away from Evair right now.

"Okay," he said, amused. He sheathed his gun, grinning at her. "Lead the way, princess."

The other hunters had a laugh, all of them putting their weapons away too. She knew that it would only take each of them a mere second to draw again, and any hint of magic from her would put Evair in danger again.

I have to get them out of this room. Maybe he can heal if he has time.

She pressed her hand to Evair's nose just once. Then she turned to join the small group. There were two women and three men, all of them hard looking with flinty eyes and sharp mouths. Every expression they made seemed full of pain. She wondered what sort of life they had to have had to enjoy inflicting suffering on others. She wished she could pity them.

"No tricks," the big guy said. She walked ahead of him towards the far wall, mentally retracing her steps from the opposite side so she could gauge the lengths of the openings and the positions of the door. She paused, listening to the sliding of stone, and feeling the vibration in the floor.

"Get moving," the big guy said. He pulled out a pistol and jabbed her in the back with it. She put her hands up immediately.

"It's up to you if you want to hold your weapon," she said calmly, "but the maze is full of pitfalls. You might find that you need both hands for other things."

She looked back at him and saw him scowling in fury. He put his gun back into his weapons belt, frowning. Penny breathed a sigh of relief, turning back to the maze.

They could shoot her at any time. She knew that. She also knew she probably wasn't going to get killed by the maze itself because she knew how it worked. Her mind raced as she tried to think of ways to get them killed but staying safe herself.

She had no idea what was waiting on the other side. The second half of the maze was probably far more dangerous than the first, and there were still two seals to go. She took a deep breath and moved forward, clenching her fists in determination.

"Stay close to me," she said to the hunters. "The doors move swiftly. I'll have to make quick decisions about which way to go. If you don't keep up, you'll be crushed, and there might be more traps set in the maze itself."

The big guy touched his gun again. "Just make sure you get us out of here, witch. Any trouble from you, and I'll go back and skin your Dragon friend myself. You got it?"

She nodded, knowing that he was going to do that at the first opportunity, anyway. She didn't want to leave Evair, but she knew it was her only choice. She was confident she could get the hunters caught in a trap and then come back for him, but would she make it in time?

"Okay," she said. "Let's go." she knew that she was stalling, and she didn't have time for this. Part of her was hoping to see Evair rise up from the floor, pull out the arrows and eat all the people two at a time. She risked a glance his way and saw his breathing had fallen to an even slower, softer rhythm. Tears burned her eyes as she turned back to the door.

She heard stone scraping and then a click. The opening appeared, and she stepped through, hurrying forward to make enough room for the hunters. She heard them scurrying to keep up, but she didn't slow down. She kept jogging towards the next door, listening to the stone scraping and locking all around her.

She looked behind her and saw the hunters running to keep up. Their eyes were fearful as they looked around and above them, waiting for traps to fall. Penny almost held her breath in anticipation… she was waiting for the exact same thing.

25
EVAIR

Pain.

Pain was the entirety of Evair's existence. It streaked through his blood, sent daggers into his muscles and crippled his joints. He tried to scream, but only a low, whispering moan came from his mighty jaws.

He struggled against the pain and the wave of consciousness that was threatening him. He was desperate to return to that abyss of icy, silent calm that existed on the other side. Anything was better than this, even death.

But something kept buzzing against Evair's brain, something irritating and relentless. He had to stay. There was a reason why he had to stay and fight. A reason that made all the pain worthwhile.

My mate.

He tried to move but only groaned again as the pain roared through his every cell. His eyelids flickered, the dim lights of the chamber feeling like they were tearing into his pupils. He just wanted to sleep. Why wouldn't the earth let him sleep?

My mate.

The thought was insistent. It had weight as well as tenacity. He fought against it. He had no mate. He had always been alone and always would be alone. There was no reason at all for him to hang on.

As he relaxed against the cold floor, letting the poison take him, images filled his mind. The flash of bright red hair. Clear, wide green eyes that sucked him in and drowned him any time he looked into them. Soft, pale skin and the curve of her red lips. He heard her laugh, felt her touch. The sensation was so real he shivered all over.

Penny!

His eyes blinked open, and this time he didn't care that the light pierced his pupils. He looked around as best he could without getting up because his body still refused to obey him. He could feel the poison as both fiery and numb. The individual arrows were embedded deep in his flesh, aching with a sharp bite as they delivered the Dragon's bane straight into his bloodstream.

The room was empty.

"Penny!" he cried, suddenly realizing the truth. The truth about everything.

Penny is my mate!

A scream ripped from Evair's throat as he forced himself to his feet. Now that his mind was returning, he remembered his brother, too, as well as other Dragons slumbering around the world that needed his help. Duty and responsibility weighed heavily on him, but above all, he wanted to find Penny, to be by her side.

He reached up and grabbed one of the arrows in his chest. He wrenched it free, roaring as it tore open his flesh. The wound bled freely as he hurled the arrow away and grabbed the next.

The hunters had done their work well. At least seven arrows were embedded in his flesh, and they were deep. Some he had to twist and pull at the same time to free them. Each time he tore an arrowhead from his flesh, he had to stop and breathe while his body trembled with the effort.

Shaking and gasping, he pulled out the last arrow. His blood was flowing across the floor like a river. He collapsed, groaning as he shuddered with pain.

Even though the wounds hurt, the throb of poison in his veins began to subside, just a little. He had absorbed a lot of it, but now that the arrows were out of his flesh, the Dragon's bane was being washed out of the wounds by his blood. He didn't try to cover any of the wounds, knowing that he could afford to lose quite a bit of blood before he weakened.

He forced himself to get to his feet. He knew that if he moved around, got his heart rate up and his breathing high, his wounds would bleed even more, and he would work the poison through. Evair had believed a dose of Dragon's bane, even in the smallest measure, to be fatal. Yet here he was, suffering from multiple wounds, but still alive.

Painfully, he turned towards the far door. He saw the opening close and then open again, remembering Penny's instructions. All he had to do was time his movements correctly, and he should make it through each door, eventually leading to Penny. The problem was, he was still very slow and heavy, and the doors moved quickly. He couldn't afford to get wounded again, or he'd never get out of here, let alone rescue Penny.

Evair swept through the first door, stumbling painfully on the other side. He caught Penny's scent straight away and followed it, bounding down the hall. The idea that she might be close and in danger obliterated thought and destroyed caution. He was too badly injured to make decisions properly and mindlessly chased the hint of scent until he found himself at a dead end.

He realized with dismay that he had followed the same corridor without looking to the sides for openings. He had probably just circled the maze on its longest, outer ring and was now somewhere close to the start.

There was no way of knowing exactly where he was, though. That was the genius nature of this maze. Once he began to run, he became lost in the never ending spiral of moving doors.

He crouched on the floor, putting his claws around his face. His head hurt now, and so did his heart. The poison burned in his veins, and his joints felt like they were being stabbed with hot pokers. Every breath was heavy, slow, and difficult. Evair didn't know how to go on.

I must, he whispered to himself. *I have to find Penny.*

Again, his mind was flooded with images of

her, but this time it was the moments when they had lain together. A soft gasp burst from his lips as he remembered their bodies coming together for the first time, the extreme sense of power and connection that he had shut himself away from.

He remembered the tattoo flaring to life across her skin. There was more proof, so much more, but this was the feeling he needed to remember.

I am mated. I have a mate, and she is here, in danger!

He thrust his feet down on the floor and reared, throwing his wings high. His voice poured from his throat in a mighty roar that shook the stone walls. Wind buffeted against him, so strong that he could hear the mountain itself groaning as it tried to contain him.

Penny.

His mind overflowed with her image, her beauty.

Penny.

His heart was filled with love, admiration, and joy.

Penny.

My love.

He screamed even louder, fighting against the poison inside him, his multitude of wounds and the futility of being stuck in this damn maze when he should be by her side.

There was a sudden snap, like the first lightning bolt just before a storm hits. Evair felt his roar die in his chest as he looked at his wings in surprise.

They were glowing.

As he watched in fascination, a white, blue glow shimmered across his scales. He was too curious to be frightened, not that he felt a need to be. The glow was warm and relaxing, even though it did prickle a bit. To his astonishment, the light healed his wounds. He watched them close one by one.

There was a thrumming in the air. It felt like the pause between lightning and thunder, and it held the same anticipation. Evair felt something in his bones, something searing and hot, like nothing he had ever felt before. It was like having a great cyclone inside him, the greatest force of wind ever known to the earth. Except this wasn't his usual power. He could feel it. This was more fierce, more brutal, and much more destructive.

He threw his wings out to the sides and screamed, pouring all of that power into the air around him. His skin hummed, and he shivered as his scales glowed and pulsed, gaining intensity by the second. The energy grew until he felt it would kill him, literally disintegrate him from the bones out to the furthest scale.

Then the crackling increased, and his body reached its limit. Lightning crackled around his claws and streaked across his body. When he roared this time, furious bolts of lightning charged down the hallway in front of him, tearing rock from the walls and scarring the floor.

He expected to be drained, even just a little tired, but instead, he was energized. He leapt forward, charging down the hallway back towards the last opening. To his dismay, he seemed to have grown a little, but he was able to maneuver even faster now.

It's like being liquid lightning! he thought, surging through the tunnels with joy. He couldn't wait to find Penny. He knew she would still be alive. She had to be. Now he could find her and destroy the Dragon hunters once and for all.

He flapped his wings and roared again, causing lightning to streak around him. It emerged from the cracks between his scales and dripped off his claws. He was astonished that this great power had lived inside him for thousands of years, and he had never known about it.

He couldn't wait to test his new limits, to fly as fast as he could and release lightning bolts of incredible intensity. As he shrugged off the pain of his previous form and embraced his new one, pure joy rose in him, an emotion he had truly never known before.

All because of Penny... all of it!

He hurried, chasing through the openings of the maze. He would be in time. She would be alright. He just knew it.

Because they were each other's destiny.

26
PENELOPE

Penny rushed through the maze, lending urgency to the five hunters that followed her. She kept them on their toes, never slowing down. She wanted them running hard and only thinking about the dangers of the maze itself.

She hurried because she wanted to get back to Evair, and she was looking for the perfect moment to escape. She also kept them moving quickly in the hope that they might screw up and end up dying in the jaws of the maze.

They were all swift and nimble, though, especially the biggest guy. He stayed right behind Penny at every step, making sure that she didn't get too far ahead. He watched her with suspicion, and that was another good reason to keep them moving quickly. She didn't want any of them to suspect she was leading them the wrong way.

If she weren't trying to rush back to Evair, she would have enjoyed such a game. The maze was deadly at every turn, and even if the traps didn't kill you, the design was meant to torture its victims into insanity. She actually laughed a little as she thought about the Dragon slayers wandering lost until they died of thirst.

There are downfalls to being fit with perfect reflexes, she thought. No matter how closely she timed her jumps around the doors, all of them still made it through. She didn't even manage to lose a few in the previous hallways.

She was gasping for breath now, her limbs heavy, and her muscles were burning. She didn't know how long she had been running, but it felt like days. She thought with longing of the binge TV session she'd discussed with Evair, letting her mind linger on the comfy bed, the big screen TV flickering against the darkness, and Evair's arms around her.

"Keep moving," the big guy said, jabbing her with his bow. She frowned, heading for the next door.

"We're almost there now," she said, breathless.

"We better be. I'm starting to suspect you aren't taking us back to the start."

She had plenty of clever retorts but just sighed. She timed their jump to the next corridor and slipped through, walking up to the wide arch that marked the exit. The hunters cheered as they came through, looking around the open space eagerly.

"Looks like we made it," one of the girls said.

"Pity about Jenkins," one of the guys muttered.

"We all knew what we were signing up for," the big guy snarled.

"What about Walker," one of the others asked. "He's fucked for life over this whole thing."

"That's what he got for listening to that fucking idiot Fetterson. We'll deal with him once we get out of here. I can tell you this, I think we're lucky to have lost so few. This is one of the worst Dragon tombs I've ever been in."

Penny stood at the entrance to the next cave, trying not to listen. They had lost members of their team at every seal, and Penny didn't like to think about the fact that such evil people could also be capable of ordinary things such as friendship. It made her sick to think that this was their work, their job, and talking about their friends dying was done with the same casual ease expressed by a retail shop girl saying, with annoyance, that a certain employee had dodged a shift.

"What now?" the big guy growled, stepping up beside Penny. She shook her head.

"I don't know."

The cavern was completely black. Across the ceiling was a faint blue glow. She called up a little ball of light and sent it high.

Across the floor in front of them were loose, grassy clods of earth. It looked impossible, like a dug-up garden existing under the earth away from the sun. Penny approached it gingerly.

The hunters came after her, pointing their guns wildly in every direction. As the light floated up to the ceiling, Penny saw Dragon runes carved across the ceiling. The spot on her stomach where the tattoo had flared to life pulsed once, and she touched the spot.

Suddenly, the runes made sense to her.

'Here lie the hungry dead.'

Penny started shuffling backwards, very slowly. She was getting seriously bad vibes from this place, and she didn't want to cross the uneven earth. It looked like it had been recently dug up, and she was afraid she knew why.

One of the women turned around, seeing Penny retreating towards the maze. She pointed her gun and yelled at her.

"Hey, you! Don't fucking disappear, what do you think you're…"

Her sentence cut off into a piercing scream as hands came up through the loose soil, grabbing her ankles. She fired wildly into the ground, falling as the hands yanked her down. She fell awkwardly, hitting her head on the butt of her gun.

Another guy screamed, fighting desperately with the hands coming up to grab at him. He pulled a large knife, hacking at the fingers. No matter how many he cut off, the hands kept coming.

"Keep moving!" roared the big guy. "Up here, there's solid rock. Nothing can crawl out of the earth up here. Just get past it."

His voice trailed away, and with a brief thought, Penny sent her orb of light towards him. The chittering sound that scratched at the edge of her consciousness was far louder now, enhanced by her fear. She kept her eyes on the darkness beyond the big guy, waiting to see what the light would reveal.

There was a terrifying moan and a scraping

sound. Penny took a few steps back, and even the big guy scuttled away. Two of the hunters were clawing their way free of the undead hands grappling with them from under the ground, but Penny feared that much worse was waiting for them on the other side of the little graveyard.

"Illuminate," she whispered. The ball of light grew, flaring like a spotlight. She let out a short, sharp scream as she saw what was advancing from the dark.

An army of the dead, hundreds of them. Some were only skeletons, still hung with armor and gripping heavy shields and swords. Others had rotting flesh hanging from their bones, with tatters of clothes remaining on them.

The chittering, chattering sound got far louder. Penny couldn't tell if the creatures were making the sound or if it was coming from somewhere else. It confused her that these things could moan because surely, they didn't have voices.

Do they? She thought in panic. *What kind of horrible magic would leave them their voices? Did that mean they were conscious?*

She staggered away, gagging. The skeletons kept moving, the noises they made scraping at her nerves. Their bones clicked as they moved, and their weapons dragged on the floor. Their eyeless faces turned towards the living humans with a horrible, purposeful intent.

The two hunters on the ground pulled themselves away from the fresher corpses and began to fire on the army of the dead. There was a cackling sound from the ranks, a spooky echo of laughter. Something screamed eagerly, and then the entire army was running at the five hunters.

Penny couldn't run. All she could do was keep sliding backward. She felt like if she made a sudden move, it would turn the undead army in her direction. She had to give the hunters credit, for they didn't run, but their attacks were all but useless.

How do you kill the dead? She thought.

The cave erupted with gunfire and screams. The big guy, the leader, had drawn a very long, broad knife and was hacking the dead to pieces. Even once they were taken down, the arms, legs and heads writhed on the ground, still seeking to kill their enemies.

Penny was almost at the door, the maze right behind her. She realized that she could get to Evair while they were distracted, and hope surged in her chest.

But how will we get out? If we come this way, we'll run into the dead army... If any of these hunters get through, then they'll have Aelon! What can we do?

She didn't even know if Evair would be alive when she got back. She swallowed her grief, unable to stop the hot tears from pouring down her cheeks.

Don't worry about anything right now. Just get to Evair.

It was sound advice. Once she got to him, she could figure out what to do. She kept her eyes on the fight ahead, wondering how big the dead army was, how many ranks would come forth to attack. She wondered if they would come through the maze and flood the passages.

Just as she turned to run, she saw the big guy turning towards her. The other hunters were all going down screaming, bullets shattering against the walls as they fired wildly, trying to save themselves. The big guy casually cut off the arm of a corpse that grabbed him and pointed his long machete at Penny. "You!" he screamed.

Penny turned and bolted back into the maze, her heart in her throat. Terror was rushing through her, making her feel desperate and weak. She didn't know what she was more afraid of, the big guy catching her, the undead catching her, or Evair being dead.

She slipped through the first opening, hearing the hunter not far behind her. She panted, waiting for the doors to move, hearing her attacker maneuvering himself to make the next jump right behind her. Penny's eyes blurred with tears as she thought of getting back to the center and finding Evair dead.

If he is, then I don't care what the hunter or the dead do to me, she thought, *helplessly. If I don't have Evair, I have nothing. If this is his grave, then it's mine too.*

The doors slammed together nearby, making her jump. The chittering grazed against her mind like a keen blade on a blackboard. The dead scraped and moaned in the next chamber as the hunter cursed, trying to follow her movements.

Doesn't matter, she thought. *All that matters is getting to Evair. Then you can kill me.*

She just wanted to hold him one more time, even if there was no life left in his body. She couldn't believe she had wasted so much time trying to convince herself that she didn't love him.

Now he was gone, and her life was over, one way or another.

She set her teeth in determination, gathering herself. She still had some power left. If Evair was dead, and she was about to be, she might just have enough energy to make sure the hunter got what he deserved, as well.

27
EVAIR

Evair dove through the narrow hallways, twisting and turning on himself like a serpent in a current. He could feel the air in a way he never had before. It was as if his entire body were buoyant and flowed through the ether without the need of his wings.

He could feel Penny getting closer and closer, knowing that his every step brought him nearer to her. He knew which door to take. He knew the direction to move towards in every corridor. As his blood grew hotter and his heart pounded faster, he let out a tremendous roar that shook the walls of the maze.

As Evair felt Penny's presence getting closer, he could sense her desperation. She was running, scared, almost out of power. He roared again, and the nearby walls shuddered so hard they let out clouds of thick, pale dust. They did not shatter, though, even when he smashed up against one in frustration. He had to marvel at the workmanship.

Then, he heard voices. One was certainly Penny, and the other was one of the hunters. He wondered where the others were. If they were backing each other up from not far away. If he dove through the next opening, he might be faced with all of them and end up skewered by dozens of arrows again.

He couldn't convince himself that caution was needed. He felt invincible. Even though he realized he most likely wasn't. He didn't feel that he could be taken down by a few hunters with Dragon's bane arrows. Not anymore.

He sensed Penny's magic rising and listened to the movement of the wall, ready for the door to open. He could smell her as well as sense her, and she was definitely on the other side of the wall. Her scent was strong with fear, and even though she spoke bravely, there was a tremble in her voice.

The wall clunked, vibrating against the floor. Only a few more seconds.

He leapt through the opening the second it

appeared, charging towards Penny and the hunter. He saw that her hands were glowing with light as she screamed at him, trying to immobilize him and push him back into the wall of the maze so he would be crushed.

She was too weak. The hunter was affected, his movements had become much slower, but he did not succumb. They fought together in the center of the corridor, struggling back and forth to gain an advantage.

Power crackled across Evair's scales. He could even smell the lightning, the too clean, burning smell of torn ozone. He opened his jaws, and sparks flew around his teeth.

He took a couple of quick steps forward, flowing up the corridor. Then Evair opened his mouth, and he neatly scooped the hunter into his mouth. He crunched twice, his massive, strong teeth slicing the hunter into scattered pieces. Evair chomped a few times, swallowing, and shook his head.

Penny was standing directly beneath him when he looked down, her hands clutched together at her chest. She gazed up at him, a faint spray of blood across her face. Her eyes were wide as she tried to take in his new form. He'd known that he was somewhat bigger than before, but now that he saw Penny looking so small and seemingly far away, he realized he was significantly larger.

"Evair?" she whispered, coming closer to reach out to him. He put out a claw towards her, and she touched his knuckle. Her hand felt warm on his cool scales.

"Penny," he whispered, and his voice was full of promise.

"What happened?" she asked. He shook his head.

"I just had to accept the truth, then I became what I truly am."

He leaned down, pressing his nose to her chest. She wrapped her arms around him immediately and pressed her body tightly against him.

"You're my mate," he whispered. Penny gasped, and he felt the warmth flooding her body as she responded to his words. She kissed him on the forehead with warm, soft lips, and power flashed through him. When he opened his eyes, he was human again, and Penny laughed in delight when he threw his arms around her and kissed her.

"You are mine, I know it," she murmured, grabbing onto his shoulders and kissing him. She pressed her body firmly against his, and there was no mistaking how fast he responded to her.

"Please, my love," he gasped. "Let me go. There is still danger, and I can't…"

She laughed, sliding her body on his teasingly. "Alright. I'll let you go, for now." She looked him up and down. "Are you going to traverse the rest of the challenges naked?" she asked.

He shrugged. "I believe I can shift at will now. But at any rate, I don't have anything to wear."

"We could strip a Dragon hunter," she said, idly, "Or one of the dead."

Evair stopped, feeling his heart slow in his chest. "The dead?" he whispered.

She sighed. "The next seal is an army of the dead. I'm pretty sure that the other hunters are dead, too. I have no idea how to get past them."

Evair took two steps forward, shifting as he went. Penny jogged to catch up as he started twisting down hallways like a minnow.

"The dead are not uncommon to use as guards," he said. "But they are almost impossible to control. They could take me down if there are enough of them."

They had reached the outer door. Evair moved through quickly, Penny right behind him. The large chamber seemed empty, the sounds of the cave echoing faintly back to them. A drip of water, rolling stone and perhaps a hint of disembodied laughter.

"They were here," she murmured. "A whole army of them."

"I can't blow them away or freeze them," Evair said. "My new lightning could fail to turn them to ash, and then they would just keep coming. Can't you do a spell?"

"Necromancy?" she asked, in alarm. "I don't have the power for that."

There was a scrape in the darkness and a moan. They both jumped, looking into the shadows.

"I'm not asking you to raise the dead, Penny," he snapped, getting desperate. "I want you to put them to sleep!"

Penny's face brightened as she put her hands together, concentrating. Raising the dead from their graves took great and terrible power. It went against nature. Putting them back in their graves was merely resetting things to their rightful place.

After a few seconds of concentrating, she reached for Evair, her hands feeling very warm on his cool scales. He felt her powers reach through him, connecting to the air and lightning that lived in his blood. Her magic was elemental, of the earth, and through him, she could reach even greater strength.

The army of the dead came shuffling and scraping out of the dark, lurching towards them. Penny began to whisper under her breath, and just when Evair thought he would have to break and fight, the dead army faltered.

They stood still, looking around. Most dropped their weapons. They began to shuffle back to the soft ground from whence they'd come, and older carcasses shuffled back still further to the massive stone chamber beyond the patch of uneven earth. The older dead had sarcophagi or stone tombs to receive them.

Evair had to wonder if the dead had been buried here or if his brother had sought out dead kings and warriors to fill his sleeping chamber. It was beyond creepy, even for a Dragon.

Still, Penny kept her head down, her hands together. She whispered gently, focusing on sending the dead back to sleep. Evair smiled as he realized that she was singing them a lullaby.

He watched old bones drag themselves underground, and the wrapped figures put themselves back in gilded boxes. Some climbed up onto horses that were perched atop stone platforms, and still others laid themselves in elaborate, stone coffins. As the last dead defender settled itself into its resting place, Penny looked up and smiled when she saw the way ahead was clear.

They started walking across the uneven ground, coming over to the massive stone chamber beyond. It was slightly unnerving to walk between the ranks of the dead in this way, but that might only be because Evair had just seen them staggering across the floor, ready to fight to protect his brother's resting place.

They approached what looked like a solid rock wall. He had no doubt the last sealing would be the worst. He thought of all the ancient powers that Dragons could command and the terrible magics that could be released upon them. He was doubting the mission now, mostly because the hunters were dead, and his brother was in no immediate danger. He didn't want to risk Penny getting hurt if he didn't have to.

Darkness fluttered across them, making Evair realize there was a glowing torch set high on the wall. It was curious, for it was up too high for even he to reach, but the flickering glow did not appear to be flame. He glanced back down to the raised platform leading up to the wall, seeing Penny about to ascend the steps to approach the wall.

He shifted quickly, enjoying the fluidity of his bones. All he needed to do was turn his attention to the other shape, and his body obeyed. He leapt forward and grabbed Penny's hand. She turned and met his eyes.

"From now on, we do everything together," he said, urgently holding her hand. She nodded.

"Together," she whispered. Evair smiled and came up the steps until they were level. He kissed her gently.

Then they turned and walked up the stairs that led to the final seal.

28
PENELOPE

The steps were large and wide. Cut straight out of the stone with incredible precision. It would have taken the finest stonemason in the world years to make such a staircase. Penny could tell by each rise of her leg that every step was identical in shape and size to the one before.

The structure was impossibly large, and Penny had vertigo before they had even made it halfway up the staircase. The stairs made a wide arc that narrowed to the small platform at the very top. She couldn't see much on the way up, but it appeared to be a dead end.

Penny held Evair's hand tightly, reassured by the fact that he could shift at will now. She was tired, drained, and knew that her magic would not save her if there was real danger. She would have to rely on Evair.

It wasn't a bad thing at all to have to rely on him, especially now that she could feel their hearts beat as one. It just gave her a growing sense of fear that the next battle would likely be the worst, and she had no strength of her own.

She glanced over at Evair and saw him smiling at her. His long, pale hair shifted in the breeze, and his eyes were like lasers as they looked into hers. She smiled and squeezed his hand as they took the next step together.

"So, what happens when we wake your brother?" she asked in a small voice. "I'm assuming that he might not be happy about it."

"He may not be," Evair agreed. "He certainly went to a lot of trouble to make sure he wouldn't be disturbed. He isn't safe here, though. More hunters will come."

"They wouldn't all survive," muttered Penny. Evair nodded.

"True. But only one needs to make it through."

Penny focused on the next step. They were just a little higher than was comfortable for her, and she had to wonder if the ascent got steeper on every step. Perhaps the final seal was to exhaust the penitent so slowly they gave up before they reached the summit.

Evair suddenly looked up towards the top, scenting the air.

"What is it?" she asked, waiting for banshees to come screaming out of the dark.

"It's getting colder," he whispered. "You feel it?"

She did. Her skin was reacting to the air as if she were in a freezing cold pool. It made it even harder to keep moving. It really did feel like the stairs were getting steeper. Maybe just being underground for so long was affecting her mind.

I could use a hot bath and a long nap, she thought. *A pile of cookies and a nice cup of tea wouldn't go astray, either.*

"Are you alright, my love?" Evair asked, squeezing her hand.

"I'm so tired," she whispered, struggling to keep her eyes open. Evair breathed out suddenly, with a sharp sound. Penny's head cleared immediately.

"What did you do?" she asked.

"I increased the oxygen in the air, just a little. I can't fix exhaustion, but that will wake up your brain a little."

She smiled, holding his hand tightly as they

headed up the next step. They were almost at the top now, and Penny felt like she was dragging herself over the final step. She didn't even want to think about getting down. She was far too tired to do it properly and would more than likely fall.

She sat on the stone floor for a few moments, taking in the view from the top of the dais. There was a small gold box on top of the stone platform and nothing else.

"What is it?" she asked as Evair looked it over.

"It may be a key or something," he said. "This box is hardly big enough to hold a cat."

"So long as Schrodinger isn't around, that should work out fine," Penny said, without thinking. She laughed at Evair's frown. He shook his head and waved a hand, no longer bothered by references he didn't yet understand.

He touched the box gently, reading the symbol. In the front were two gold keys set at either end.

"I believe that only fated mates can turn the keys," he said. "Some of these Dragon runes are beyond my understanding, but I think if we turn them at the same time, we should open the box. Then we'll know how to awaken my brother."

"And if you're wrong?"

Evair shrugged. "Certain death."

Penny giggled, her mind instantly bringing up a scene from *Labyrinth*.

"Hopefully, we get to dance with David Bowie," she giggled.

"Is now really the time?" Evair snapped. Penny groaned as she got up.

"It's always a good time to make light of the situation," she said, looking him in the eye. "My Dad taught me that."

Evair looked humbled and turned his eyes back to the mysterious box. She went to the other end, and they both touched the keys at the same time.

"Ready?" he whispered. "We must turn at the same time, so the tumblers align at the same instant. One, two, three."

They both turned their keys. There was a clunking sound and a rumble far beneath their feet. For a few seconds, it felt like the mountain was going to come apart beneath them. Penny was so shocked she could barely move. Evair reached for her as a violent shudder brought them both to their knees. They managed to grab each other's hands as they were hurled from the top of the dais.

Penny felt Evair's arms go around her as they rolled from the top step. She wreathed them in a light protection spell, but she couldn't stop them from falling. Even though neither of them was badly hurt, she felt every single stair on the way down as they bounced off each one.

When they finally reached the floor and rolled across it to a messy, tangled up stop, they both looked at the stone steps in shock. The mountain was moving, vibrating, crumbling. It was shaking as if something large were rising from underneath it.

"Oh, shit," muttered Evair.

The stone steps shattered, shards of rock flying around the chamber like bullets. Something screamed, and Penny saw bright blue wings unfolding through the crumbling artifice.

"He was buried underneath it!" she screamed.

They both jumped up and ran back towards the hallway of the dead, but all they found was a dead end. A great wall of stone had come down, cutting them off from the way they had come in. Evair turned in panic, watching the shape of his brother rising from the rock.

"Oh, no," he whispered, looking around. "We're sealed in."

"But he's your brother!" Penny screamed. "He'll recognize you, won't he?"

"He might," Evair said. "But that's not the problem. The problem is…"

A rushing sound suddenly overtook the crumbling, shattering noise of stone. It sounded to Penny like she was standing by a turbulent ocean or rapid stream. It was somewhat soothing… Except that it was getting louder.

"In elemental magic, the only thing that defeats air is water," Evair whispered.

"What?" screamed Penny. "What are you talking about?"

Evair ran towards the hill of crumbling stone. Penny could see wings, horns and a long neck struggling up from where the creature had rested for thousands of years. He had been sealed in by the exquisite stonework, completely entombed so securely that even he could not get out unless the keys were turned. It was taking him some time to free himself from the stone.

"Aelon!" screamed Evair. "Can you hear me?"

The Dragon roared. The sound of the rocks falling increased, and so did the rushing sound. Cracks began to appear across the floor, bleeding out from the stone staircase, which had been almost completely reduced to rubble.

"Aelon!" Evair yelled again. "Brother, it's me!"

The Dragon under the rock roared, a sound of fury and savagery. The rushing sound got louder, and suddenly, Penny knew what it was.

Small streams of water began to run from the cracked stone. The Dragon shrieked, water and rock flowing down towards Penny and Evair. The water gathered strength, trickling faster and faster. The roaring noise got so loud it drowned out the shattering sound of stone.

Penny began to take slow steps back. Soon, she met the blank wall that kept them from retreating into the maze. Evair hammered on it, but it had fallen into place so securely it looked like it had stood for eons, not hours.

There was a tremendous crack along the full length of the stone tower. The Dragon roared, and the sound of water rushing got even louder.

"He's a Water Dragon," Penny croaked, barely able to breathe. "He's a Water Dragon, and we're sealed in!"

Evair reached for her, wrapping his arms around her. The final stones cracked open with a sound worse than thunder, releasing the water in a roaring, unstoppable force. Aelon broke free from the pyramid, shattering the last vestiges of his stone prison as he spread his wings and screamed in the glory of his freedom.

Penny only had a few seconds to see the towering shape, adorned in dark blue and lots of long spines, before the water hit them. She tried to hold on to Evair, but the force was too strong, and they were ripped apart.

She was tossed against the stone walls and tumbled through the waves. She couldn't tell which way was up.

The chamber would fill up. Aelon had guarded his resting place well. Even if someone could beat all the seals, they would still die. Aelon had been buried in his element, and now that he was awake, it would murder anyone who dared disturb him.

She struggled through the water, blind and slow. Just when she thought she couldn't hold on any longer, and she would have to inhale air, she felt hands on hers.

Evair!

His lips touched hers, and suddenly her lungs were full of air. She pressed herself against him, drinking life from his lips as he kicked upwards, bringing them to the top of the water. They were not far from the roof, and the water was still filling the chamber.

Aelon roared under the water, charging them. Evair squeezed Penny's hand.

"When I shift, I'll create an explosion of air. It will force the water from the room, then I will try to reach my brother. Be ready."

Without another word, he kicked away from her. The water began to spiral around him as Aelon approached. Penny hugged her arms around herself and called up whatever power she had left.

Evair shifted, and water and air met in the chamber, the pressure exploding webs of pressure cracks across the walls where the water began to escape. As the underground sea began to fall, Evair locked eyes with Aelon. Penny gasped as the water level fell, praying that Evair could reach his brother before it came to an all out battle.

29
EVAIR

As his brother swung around to meet his gaze, Evair wished he could shift into his original form. Not that he would want to give up his new strength and power, no, but because Aelon might be more likely to recognize him that way.

Yet, Aelon stopped as he registered the presence of another Dragon. He banked in the water, even as the level of it fell around them. Evair's brother roared once more, but the sound was no longer filled with rage. Instead, it was the challenge of a Dragon on his own territory to a newcomer, demanding the visitor announce himself.

"I am your brother, Evair!" The pearlescent

Dragon tried to bellow, but the waves were still above his head, and the words came out as garbled bubbles of air.

Evair cast a look over his shoulder at Penelope, his heart hammering. There was a faint glow about her that reassured him. She had dug deep into her reserve of energy and cast one more spell that was keeping her breathing.

Knowing that Penny was alright for the time being sent Evair surging to the surface of the water. The walls were crumbling, allowing the interior sea to drain all the more quickly. He burst into the air, his whole body free of the waves.

Aelon followed, shrieking a new and more threatening challenge. Evair had left his brother's element, which could be construed as an attempt to cause an insult. As soon as Aelon's crest breached the surface, Evair began shouting. The deep boom of his Dragon voice bounced from the stones.

"It is me, Evair! Your brother! Aelon, you know me, 'tis I. Evair!"

Hovering opposite Evair, Aelon cocked his head.

"Evair?" He blinked luminous silver eyes. "My brother was not so large. But you have his voice…"

"I am mated," said Evair hastily. "In accepting my mating bond, I came into my final form. I can prove I am Evair, listen, our mother was Arindel, our father Pelosoph, we have two more brothers…"

"Enough!" Aelon snorted amusement. "I believe you, I believe you. Only a mated pair could free me against my will. And you smell as you always have, like the winter wind. Although there is a new layer of ozone now… interesting. You say your mating bond caused this?"

Evair could not help but let out a Dragon's laugh, a sound like gemstones tumbling against each other and the trumpeting of golden horns.

"Now is not the time to analyze, Aelon," he said before diving back down to the water for Penelope. The flood was barely eight feet tall now. As Evair shot towards where he felt Penny to be, the top of her head broke through the foaming waters.

"A human!" Aelon snapped his wings together and went into a dive himself. "I was right. There are Dragon hunters here!"

"She's my mate! Did you not listen to what I just told you?" Evair landed with a splash, fanning out his wings to buoy Penelope slightly. She gasped, and the gentle light around her dissipated immediately.

"Your mate is *human*?" Aelon landed with a second smaller splash. Evair was surprised to realize that he and his brother had been of a size before. Now he practically dwarfed his sibling.

"Penny," murmured Evair, ignoring his brother's question to focus on his trembling mate. "My love, are you alright?"

"I'm... very... very... tired," announced Penelope, her cherished voice breathier than usual. Then, her eyes rolled up into the back of her head, and she fainted.

"Aelon, can you clear away the rest of this water?" barked Evair, keeping Penelope balanced on his wing. "Now!"

To his credit, Aelon did so right away. Slow and smooth, the water receded away, creating an ever growing dry circle around Evair and Penelope. Evair shifted, catching Penny in human arms as his feet met solid ground.

He cradled her damp form to his chest, feeling her pulse beating reassuringly. It was a touch weaker than usual, but the difference could be accounted for by magic exhaustion. Her face was white, and Evair recalled what she'd told him about how magically overextending herself made her feel nauseated.

Aelon drew closer to them, shrinking into his own human form with an effortlessness that Evair envied after so long being unable to shift at will. His brother's silver eyes glowed with curiosity as he examined Penelope.

"A human mate! Fascinating. I have never read of such a thing, but I can sense the bond between you." Aelon looked as though he should be wearing glasses to push up his nose. "I wish to hear the entire story, Evair."

"In due time," replied Evair, fondness coming into his voice. He remembered his brother's hunger for knowledge well. "For now, I must take care of my mate."

"Can you not revive her through the bond?" Aelon drew a little nearer, frowning with contemplation. "Sharing energy is a well known aspect of the mating bond… between two Dragons at least."

Evair felt foolish. He'd already shared energy with Penny to boost her spells. Of course, he could offer her a more generalized form.

Concentrating, he willed the light of his own soul to expand into Penelope. He'd expected a struggle, but it was shockingly easy. He had merely to reach to meet Penny's essence with his own. Fluid and natural, his energy flowed into Penny. Almost at once, her pulse strengthened, and pink returned to her cheeks.

"Oh, my." Penny's eyes fluttered open, and Evair felt his tension drain away. "Whatever you just did is much better than caffeine."

"Penny!" Evair crushed her to him, nuzzling her hair and pressing a kiss to her temple. "You fainted. I did not like it."

"Me neither, love, trust me," Penny said, her words muffled against his torso. "But I'm alright now. You healed me. You can put me down."

Evair set his mate down gingerly, keeping one hand against the small of her back to support her. Seeing that she was steady on her feet, he let his hand slide down to take hers. He lifted his head, beaming with pride as he met Aelon's interested gaze.

"You mated, Evair," commented his brother, smirking a little. "I could not have imagined it, not in all that I dreamt while under the pyramid."

"Well, I never imagined being mated to a Dragon," said Penny reasonably. "Surprises for us all, I suppose."

Aelon stared at her, then burst out laughing.

"I like her! I am very glad to see you, brother, and meet your human mate. But perhaps you will tell me why you disrupted my rest?"

"You were right that the Dragon hunters were here, brother," rumbled Evair. "They are here no longer, thanks to the efforts of Penelope and me. Yet we have discovered that there is a great cadre of them, actively hunting down our kin, so we had to wake you lest you remain vulnerable."

"I see." Aelon took a few steps closer, reaching out to clasp his brother's shoulder. "Then I thank you, Evair of the NetherVale clan, and you, Penelope, of the?"

"Cloverlid," supplied Penny, even as she averted her eyes from Aelon's nude frame. "Um, Evair. You and your brother are both, um, very, very naked. Perhaps we could continue this conversation elsewhere? Ideally somewhere with clothes?"

"If it troubles you, I will shift." Aelon shrugged, and in a heartbeat, he was the same blue Dragon that had first met them in that place.

"Wait 'til you meet your mate," muttered Evair, irrationally annoyed by Aelon's ease of shifting.

"What did you say?" Aelon blinked, genuinely asking.

"Nothing." Evair smothered a grin and turned

to the woman who had been worth every ounce of shifting frustration and more. "Penelope, my love, will you be so good as to welcome both my brother and me into your home while we plan how to best aid our kin?"

"Evair." Penny put her hands on her hips, smiling mischievously. "I don't know much about Dragon mating bonds, but I'm pretty sure the only home I have is now ours."

Overcome by emotion, Evair swept Penny into his arms. He pressed his lips to hers, feeling the same magic suffusing his veins as the very first time they kissed. He didn't think it would ever go away, as his love could only grow for this incredible woman.

"So... does that mean entry is denied me?" Aelon looked crestfallen. "I understand. You are newly mated. But I had so hoped to see a modern human dwelling from the inside."

Penny broke away from Evair, even though the desire in her eyes promised more soon enough.

"You are, *of course*, welcome in my home," she assured Aelon, who perked up instantly at her words. "As long as you need to stay, you can. Well, and as long as you, um, wear some clothes."

"I see clothes are very important to humans

still," observed Aelon. "Even my excellent memory could barely record all the fashions of years past. But there must be other changes since I have slept. What century is it? Are there any new exciting innovations?"

Evair and Penelope exchanged a look, amusement dancing in both their eyes.

"Just wait and see, Aelon." Evair chuckled and took a step away from Penelope. With room to shift, he did so, his body elongating into his new yet fundamentally familiar form. "I think you will find there is enough 'innovation' in the world these days to satisfy even your voracious curiosity."

"Then let us go out into that world!" Aelon launched himself into the air and spat a jet of water at the nearest wall. It crumbled, revealing pre-dawn light filtering through a Dragon sized hole.

"We must make haste," said Aelon, beckoning them with his wing. "We have only a little time to fly before we can be seen."

"I think I might have enough energy for an invisibility spell." Penelope put her hand on Evair's hide. The warm rightness of her touch saturated his every scale. "Are you ready to go home, my love?"

"You are my home, Penelope Cloverlid," murmured Evair. "Wherever you are, I belong."

The deepest love swirled in Penny's eyes as she pressed her lips to Evair's neck. Without needing to exchange another word, he knelt so she could climb onto his back.

Penelope settled onto Evair's back as easily as though they'd traveled together as one for a thousand years. Happiness flooded every fiber of Evair's being as he and his mate soared up into the dawn.

30
PENELOPE

The sheets rustled against Penny's naked body as she turned over in bed. The light was a pale grey, luminous shadow. It was either very early or after dawn on a very cloudy, murky day.

She reached out across the smooth mattress, searching for Evair. After the great battle and the final feat of saving Aelon, they had practically dragged themselves back to her place, where all parties had promptly collapsed.

Penny didn't know how long she had been asleep, but her eyelids and limbs were still incredibly heavy. She didn't think she had ever been through so much stress in her entire life. Even so, she felt that she ought to be sorer than she was.

Her muscles should ache, and her fingers twist in pain, but none of that was true.

She was tired, but that might just have been from tangling herself with Evair all night. A new, vigorous kind of strength welled inside her. It made her long for her lover again as she searched for him among the covers with tentative fingers.

Her eyes snapped open as she realized that Evair was not in bed with her. She sat up suddenly, looking around the room in alarm. For a moment, she thought the entire adventure had been a dream and was struck by sick horror. The grazes on her hands and the blisters on her feet protested against this theory, though.

There was a light footstep in the hall, and the door pushed open slowly, revealing Evair, his nakedness barely covered by a short silk robe. One of hers! He carefully balanced a tray on one hand, focusing completely on his step and holding the tray, so he didn't drop it.

He grinned as he approached, holding the tray in such a violent death grip that it shook. There was a tall cup of hot coffee, a pair of crispy waffles and a little vase holding a single pink rosebud. Penny was so astonished she could barely speak.

As Evair leaned forward to place the tray on the

bedside table, the short robe slid up his thighs, revealing his buttocks. Penny giggled, hiding it behind her hand.

"You are amused, my love?" he asked, kissing her gently.

"You are aware that it's women's clothing?" she laughed. He stroked the silky red lapel.

"I figured it must be, but the color is very me," he said with a smile of amused pride. She giggled again.

"Just don't bend over in public, and you'll be fine," she said, reaching for the coffee. Evair frowned, confused.

"Why would I wear such a garment in public?"

Penny shook her head, sipping the coffee. She found it good and was surprised that Evair had made it himself.

"You made this?" she asked. He nodded, smiling broadly.

"I have been watching the YouTube," he said in careful, affected speech. "Apparently, this is the height of modern romance, to bring one's lover coffee and breakfast in bed."

"Was it not a done thing in the dark ages then?" she asked, sipping the coffee. He frowned.

"I suppose I might have asked a servant to do it

once or twice. It's not something we've actually discussed. Why don't you have servants?"

She shook her head. "You need more YouTube to understand this modern world, I think."

He nodded, biting into a waffle. "I don't doubt that."

"Where's Aelon?"

"Around. He didn't exactly tell me, but he will most likely want to stretch his wings."

"So, we are alone?" She asked hopefully. He grinned.

"Yes, my love. We are alone."

She put the coffee down, reaching for him. She opened the robe, running her fingers over his smooth chest. He pulled the blankets down, revealing her nakedness. Penny didn't even remember pulling off her dirty clothes before falling into bed.

Penny moaned as he slid forward, pressing her back against the pillows. He kissed her harder and deeper, making her body awaken. She grabbed his shoulders and pulled him down on top of her, wrapping her legs around him.

For a moment, they wrestled. Evair laughed out loud between kisses, wrapping his arms around her waist as she flipped them over. She squirmed on top of him, loving the eager noises he made to encourage her.

She sat up, stretching her arms over her head. Evair made a small sound, almost a painful one. She looked down and saw his eyes open wide as if his pupils were trying to drink her in. She felt him getting harder underneath her and slid back and forth to tease him further.

He reached up, grabbing her hips. She saw ferocity surge through him, a brief moment where his eyes flared electric blue, and his lips peeled back to show his teeth. She laughed in delight as he grabbed her upper arms and hurled her down, pressing her into the mattress with his body.

He covered her mouth with deep, sensual kisses while his hands stroked her hips and thighs. She was moaning with need as he teased her still further, and when he thrust his hips forward to join them together, she ground against him eagerly, urging him on.

Penny's back bowed, her head rocked back. A strangled cry forced itself from her throat as she felt him sink into her, one thrust taking him right to the end of her. She clung to him, her nails digging into his skin as she squirmed, feeling his hardness being squeezed by her deepest muscles.

She looked up at him, reaching out to stroke his cheek. He smiled and moved his hips back and forth, very slowly, savoring every inch of her. She linked her arms around him and reached up with her lips.

When his hot, wet mouth met hers, she cried out, the sound muffled by his tongue. Her hips screwed from side to side without her conscious will, and tremors fluttered madly up and down her spine. Evair seemed to slow down, both his hands and his kisses. Penny's lust was rising swiftly, and his slow pace burned against her, making her even hotter.

Evair laughed softly as he felt her hips increase their speed, and her hands groping at his ass under the short silk robe. He pinned her hard against the mattress and treated her to incredibly long, slow strokes. Her cries rose in her throat until it sounded like long, drawn out screams.

Thank God we're home alone! She thought. Evair brought out a side to her that she had never seen. He didn't just take her body to new heights but freed her spirit as well.

As Evair drew out each stroke, she felt her body humming like a drawn bow. Her heart pounded up into her throat, and her skin felt hot. She waited for Evair to relax, and when he finally did, she grabbed his shoulders and flipped them over, grinding back and forth with swift, short strokes that quickly brought on her first orgasm.

After Evair's slow teasing, it exploded between her legs like the first surge of a volcano. Again, her voice broke free from her, and she knew her scream was ringing off the walls. She gripped him with her knees and ground downwards even harder, moaning in joy as his thick, hard cock pressed into the very end of her and brought forth another orgasm, twice as strong as the last.

Breathing heavily, she leaned forward, collapsing against his chest. His heart hammered against her cheek as she lay, gasping with effort. She was shimmering with sweat, overheated with desire but nowhere near done.

She felt Evair's hands moving on her sides, sliding around to her lower back and reaching down to cup her ass. His touch only inflamed her more, and she squirmed, exclaiming suddenly at the feel of him shifting deep inside her.

She sat up, digging her hands into his shoulders so hard that her nails pricked him. She drove her knees into his sides, sitting up just enough to swing between the two points. Her clitoris was firmly pressed between his body and hers, every last inch of her filled by his massive, hard cock. She closed her eyes briefly to savor the sensation then began to rub herself back and forth.

Her deepest muscles clenched around Evair, making him cry out. He didn't move, keeping his hips raised up so she could control the pressure. Her hands and knees dug even tighter into him as she arched her back and thrust down with her hips, hitting every sensitive spot at once.

The orgasm took her by surprise with its force. It shuddered down her spine and through every limb, bringing her skin alive with a billion tiny prickles. She heard the scream leaving her throat but didn't really associate it with herself as her pussy convulsed hard enough to make her feel bruised inside and out.

Her limbs and joints went loose like water. She felt Evair gently lowering her to the bed, cupping her breasts, stroking her belly, and gently teasing her clit. Her eyelids fluttered open, and when she saw his look of admiration. It tugged on her heart.

"I love you," she whispered, knowing that truer words had never left her lips.

"I love you," he said firmly. His eyes held a look of wonder as if he had never expected to hear himself say that. They stared into each other's eyes as their bodies sang, a resonance of perfect harmony.

Even as they did, a shimmering new light burst forth inside her. A swelling of consciousness that lit up every porch and crevice of her spirit. The gentle suffusion of her various powers coalesced into something larger. Almost terrifyingly pure.

Mating with Evair had elevated him to his highest form, but how she experienced that same level of becoming. As if the whole of her life up to that moment had been a cocoon, and now she emerged as her true self. Whatever abilities she had cultivated and honed sprang into a new, dazzling sharpness.

How did I ever think I was whole before? Penny thought. Her entire life had been spent in anticipation of being alone because she believed that no one could truly know her or understand her.

As she fell into Evair's eyes, she knew there was no doubt and no fear. What she felt in her heart was true, echoed back to her by the beat in his own chest. Their hearts were meant to be together, an echo that could outlive time.

Her skin crackled with energy, and as Evair traced his broad, strong fingers over her, she knew he could feel it too. It was impossible that he couldn't. They were part of each other in ways she could never have imagined possible. His strength was hers, and hers was his.

She grinned, reaching for him again, pressing her lips against his. The future was waiting, and destiny would be fulfilled, but first, Penny had to learn every inch of her lover's skin and satisfy him as thoroughly as he had satisfied her.

With the fresh tempest unleashed inside her, she smiled to herself, knowing that the lover beneath her was unprepared for what she was about to do to him.

ABOUT THE AUTHOR
AVA HUNTER

Hey! I'm Ava Hunter and I've been writing stories my whole life. They always somehow end up with a sexy alien or with a paranormal twist. Or both. This encourages me to write more, because why not? I'm an all-in fan of alien shows and can usually be found binge watching them as well as paranormal ones on TV when I'm not writing.

I love to bake and eat. Or just eat. Eating's my favorite. I don't discriminate but tend to stick to sweets. My happiest moments are spent reading, eating and taking long walks in nature. And of course, spending time with my favorite guy.

I worked in the business world for so long, I couldn't believe I could write in my sweats for a living. Now, it's impossible to get me out of them and into dressy stuff.

Keep up with all my new books and releases or news or just what I ate for dinner by following me on Facebook, Amazon and PLEASE sign up for my newsletter.

Newsletter sign up: https://www.subscribepage.com/avahunter

Website: https://avahunterbooks.com/

Email: avahunterwrites@gmail.com

ABOUT THE AUTHOR

New York Times and USA Today Bestselling Author

Hi! I'm Milly Taiden. I love to write sexy stories featuring fun, sassy heroines with curves and growly alpha males with fur. My books are a great way to satisfy your craving for paranormal romance with action, humor, suspense and happily ever afters.

I live in Florida with my hubby, our son, and our fur babies: Speedy, Stormy and Teddy. I have a serious addiction to chocolate and cake.

I love to meet new readers, so come sign up for my newsletter and check out my Facebook page. We always have lots of fun stuff going on there.

Find out more about Milly Taiden here:

Email: milly@millytaiden.com
Website: http://www.millytaiden.com

You can find a complete list of all my books by series and reading order at my website: milly-taiden.com

SIGN UP FOR MILLY'S NEWSLETTER FOR LATEST NEWS! http://eepurl.com/pt9q1

Made in the USA
Middletown, DE
02 December 2024